WEDDING CAKES AND WISHES

LATTES AND LEVITATION - BOOK 6

CHRISTINE POPE

WEDDING CAKES AND WISHES

Copyright © 2024 by Christine Pope

ISBN: 978-1-946435-69-9

Published by Dark Valentine Press

Cover design by Romancepremades.com.

Ebook formatting by Indie Author Services

CHAPTER 1

Thrill of the Chase

"**R**eady for this, Skye?" my best friend Deanne asked.

I nodded, even as my heart rate sped up a little. You'd think after performing this same silly charade for the past five-plus months, I'd be a little more used to the way I had to make my escape from Levitation Latte, my coffee shop in the heart of Las Vegas, New Mexico's historic downtown, but apparently not.

"Ready," I told her, hoping that saying the word out loud would make the next couple of seconds a little easier.

She opened the back door to the shop and I bolted out, heading for Max's black Ford Bronco as it came the wrong way down the alley. Sometimes Max came to pick me up from work, and other times it was either Lou D'Amato or Al Torres, his two bodyguards. They switched up at irregular intervals, doing their best to throw off the paparazzi who'd been dogging Max and me ever since word of our engagement had leaked last November. Usually, they'd all three head out at the same time, forcing the photographers to choose who they had to follow. Two of them would drive around town, leading the paparazzi on a wild goose chase, while the third person would come to get me...and I never knew who it was until I opened the back door at the end of each day.

I sincerely hoped the paps would get tired of all this after our wedding was a done deal, but with ten days to go until the big event, I knew this wasn't over yet.

Not by a long shot.

Purse strap clutched in one hand, I ran down the back steps and practically leaped into the passenger seat of Max's Bronco, which he'd pushed open for me as he rolled to a stop. Or maybe it was more of a pause, since he didn't halt his progress completely, and sped up again even as I fastened my seatbelt.

Good thing, too, because I spied the red Jeep Wrangler of one of the more determined paparazzi, a man from L.A. named Nathan O'Rourke, already barreling toward us from the other end of the alley.

But Max had taken more than his fair share of

stunt-driving classes to prepare for the numerous action films he'd starred in, and that meant we were out of that alley and careening around a corner before the red Wrangler had a prayer of catching up with us. If we were being chased by Russian agents or CIA operatives, I might have been worried that Mr. O'Rourke would have called some of his partners in crime to let them know which route we were taking back to the ranch. However, since all the paparazzi were competing with each other to get the best shot of Max Sullivan and his fiancée, I knew I didn't have to worry about that level of coordination among our stalkers.

And although Max's ranch on the east end of town technically only had one way in—a long gravel lane that branched off from the main road— you could come in from the back if you had a decent four-wheel-drive vehicle.

That was why we instead turned onto the feeder road that led to the general aviation airport about a half-mile away, then bumped along over open land for about a quarter-mile before reaching the ranch's back gate. Max had clearly already planned this angle of approach with Lou, because the older man was waiting for us there, and opened the gate to let us in before he clanged it shut and locked it up tight.

A couple hundred yards of bouncing over the barely graded track that led to the garage, and then we were safely inside, with the garage door closing behind us.

"Figures it would be O'Rourke today," Max commented as he opened his car door. "Guy just doesn't know when to quit."

"It doesn't seem like any of them do," I replied, and climbed out of the Bronco, my fingers still tightly clutched around my purse strap. Maybe once I was inside, I'd be able to truly relax.

Maybe.

Incongruously, Max grinned. Then again, while I wouldn't exactly call him an adrenaline junkie, I got the distinct impression he was having fun with all this, that it thrilled him to no end to give the paparazzi the slip day after day. I wished I could feel the same way about the situation, but at least I knew I was in good hands when he whisked me away from work. Driving into town wasn't as much of an issue; I started my day at the coffee shop so early that the celebrity photographers couldn't be bothered to chase me down at such ungodly hours of the morning, especially since they knew Max wouldn't be with me during those times.

"O'Rourke is the worst, though," Max said. By then, we'd left the garage and entered the kitchen, and although it was way too early for Lou to have started preparing dinner—the two of us generally traded that particular duty, since we both loved to cook—it still felt comforting just to be in the space, with its gleaming granite counters and the big Wolf stove that I loved almost as much as I loved Max. "Yesterday, Al caught him driving that damn Jeep of his around the perimeter, trying to figure out exactly where we've been getting in."

"Isn't that trespassing?" I asked, trying to quell a shiver. No, it wasn't as if Nathan O'Rourke was going to do anything except snag some photos of us, but still, that back route onto the ranch had been our ace in the hole, our way of knowing we could always get safely home even if there was a horde of paparazzi and their vehicles clustered at the "official" entrance to the ranch.

"It is," Max replied, his expression still cheerful. "And Al let him know all about it. Said if he caught him doing that again, we'd make sure he spent the night in jail."

And I had no doubt that Nathan O'Rourke would get to cool his heels in a jail cell if he didn't back off. Marie DeVargas, the local police chief, was an extremely no-nonsense sort, and already had a dim view of the celebrity photographers who appeared to have taken up permanent residence in Las Vegas for the past five months. They'd gotten more than their fair share of parking tickets while here, and, even though her deputies appeared to turn a blind eye to all the traffic laws Max and Lou and Al had to break while getting me safely home, they didn't seem to have any problems giving the photographers tickets for going even five miles an hour over the speed limit.

Because of that, I was pretty certain Chief DeVargas would make sure Nathan O'Rourke—or anyone else caught trespassing on Max's ranch—spent the maximum allowable amount of time locked up before posting bail.

"Well, let's hope it's deterrent enough," I said.

Without replying, Max went over to the fridge, got out a half-drunk bottle of chardonnay, and poured us each a modest glass. "Here," he told me. "It looks like you could use this."

That I definitely could. And because the weather had been cooperating lately, and had been mild and warmer than usual for this time of year, I didn't have a problem with drinking some white wine...hence, the bottle that had already been partially consumed just the day before.

"Thank you," I said gratefully, and took a sip. "Once again, you read my mind."

His blue eyes twinkled. You'd think after living with him for the past five months, I might have gotten a little more used to the brilliant flash of those eyes, the charm of his easy grins, but nope...I was just as besotted with him now as I'd been when I was nothing more than the awkward girl next door back in high school.

"I don't need to read your mind when your

face is pretty much an open book," he replied, still smiling.

True. I never would have made much of a poker player. Rather than comment on my too-revealing expression, I settled for taking another sip of wine.

When Max spoke again, though, he sounded a lot more serious. "Maybe you should think about closing the shop now, rather than waiting until next week. Everyone knows what's going on with all these damn photographers, so I doubt they'd give you too much grief."

I wasn't so sure about that...people tended to get tetchy when deprived of their morning jolt of caffeine, although there were other coffee shops around town where they could get their fix if necessary. But people were creatures of habit, and I knew they'd prefer to buy their coffee and muffins where they always did, rather than have to go out of their way to a different venue.

"The shop is fine," I said, hoping I sounded neutral. "I've got Gordon there to keep an eye on things. It's the coming and going that's the problem."

Gordon Shaw was some hired muscle Max had contracted specifically to keep an eye on the coffee shop and make sure the paparazzi didn't hound me while I was at work all day. During the winter, he'd taken over the table closest to the front door, since even he couldn't really stomach standing outside in sub-freezing temperatures for hours on end, but now that the weather had turned nice, he'd gone back to standing by the entrance for long stretches, only coming inside when he needed to take a break or grab something to eat. While he couldn't specifically bar the paparazzi from entering the shop to get a cup of coffee or whatever, all it took was one menacing glance toward the oversized cameras they carried to make it abundantly clear he'd have no problem disposing of said cameras if they were lifted even an inch in my direction. Because of that, they were on their very best behavior when they were being helped by Deanne and me.

"Maybe," Max said, not sounding very convinced. "But still, it seems like they're getting more aggressive. I'd feel better if you were here at the ranch most of the time and only went into town when you had an appointment or something."

Now, with the wedding a mere ten days away, those "appointments" were piling up fast. Deanne was working as my wedding coordinator, because wedding planners were kind of in short supply in Las Vegas and I couldn't think of anyone I trusted more to handle all the minutiae. However, I'd hired a woman named Andie Ingram to manage the catering and cake duties, since all that was definitely outside Deanne's wheelhouse. Andie was twenty-nine, a year younger than me, someone I'd found because she'd been listed in an online article in the *Santa Fe New Mexican* as one of New Mexico's top five up-and-coming chefs. Born in Albuquerque, she was currently based in Santa Fe, and the menu she'd created for the reception sounded absolutely to die for, with brie and fig crostini as one of the appetizers and red wine braised short ribs as the beef selection for the main course.

Anyway, I had meetings with Andie, fittings at the bridal shop in Santa Fe—I loved Las Vegas, but none of the local wedding stores had anything suitable for a wedding that involved one of the world's biggest box-office stars—meetings with the staff at the Plaza Hotel, whose Ilfeld Ballroom would be the site of both the service and the reception to follow. That was convenient, actually, because the Plaza was only steps away from Levitation Latte, and I could have Gordon accompany me on my visits there to keep the paparazzi at bay.

Still, it wasn't the same as staying at the ranch all day and only leaving in the company of one of Max's bodyguards. And while part of me understood the wisdom of his suggestion that I close down the coffee shop earlier than I'd planned, the other part wanted to dig in her heels and say no way.

"If I do that," I said, "isn't it kind of like giving in, like letting them know they've won?"

At once, Max set down his wine glass and came over so he could slip a reassuring arm around my waist. He smelled wonderful, as usual, of the citrusy Hermès cologne he tended to wear whenever the weather turned warmer, and I breathed him in, feeling my jangled nerves begin to settle a bit.

"It's not a battle," he said quietly. "It's more... deciding what's best for everyone concerned. I know you feel it's your responsibility to keep the shop open as long as possible, but...."

The words trailed off, as if he knew he was treading on some very unsteady ground.

Which he was. Over the past few months, I'd started to question my commitment to Levitation Latte, to wonder if it would even be feasible to keep it open after Max and I were married. The paparazzi were a constant annoyance, like a swarm of gnats that had decided to park themselves over a favorite picnic spot until the last morsel of the meal was consumed, but it was more than that. Being Max Sullivan's wife meant I would never have to worry about money again. That wasn't the reason why I was marrying him, of course, but I also couldn't ignore that my financial status was going to change enormously in the very near future.

Against the advice of his agent, his lawyer, and his accountant, he'd steadfastly refused to have me sign a prenup, saying we didn't need such a thing when we were going to be together for the rest of our lives. Most people thought he was crazy for doing so, but that was just Max. He knew how much I loved him...knew how much he loved me. Breaking up just wasn't a possibility.

At any rate, the income I earned running the coffee shop was basically what he spent each year on the housekeeper at his house in Bel-Air, so there was no reason for me to keep working...well, except the part where I wasn't sure I knew what I'd do with myself if I didn't have to get up every weekday at four-thirty to bake muffins and pastries.

All right, that wasn't completely true. Max had already told me he wished I could go with him on his film shoots, that he hated the idea of leaving me behind while he was gone for a month or more at a time. And, since he'd taken me to Paris for New Year's after a homey Christmas here in Las Vegas, I'd already had my appetite for travel more than whetted. Maybe that was because we'd flown first class and stayed in a five-star hotel, and everything had been quietly and elegantly handled for us from the moment we landed on the tarmac at Charles de Gaulle to the time we flew back to the United States, but still.

Getting to see the world at Max's side was very tempting...and something I definitely couldn't do while working full-time at Levitation Latte.

"I'm not sure I want to make a decision about

this right now," I said, and he bent down and pressed his lips gently against my hair.

"You don't have to," he replied. "I just want you to be happy."

"I *am* happy," I protested, and he smiled again, although this time, his smile was tinged with concern.

"You are," he agreed. "But I can tell you're tense. You shouldn't be stressing right now. I want you to be able to enjoy the process, not have to keep looking over your shoulder all the time."

Not sure how I should respond, I instead reached for my glass of wine and took another sip. True, most brides would agree that the run-up to a wedding could be stressful, but Max and Deanne had done their best to ensure the process went as smoothly as possible. The bridal store in Santa Fe was top-notch, and Andie Ingram was a force of nature, someone who'd also assured me that I wouldn't have to worry about a single thing, that the reception would go off without a hitch.

Problem was, Andie didn't have the power to keep the paparazzi away, and neither did Max. He'd done his best to erect what barriers he could, but even a box-office star didn't have the power to have all those gossip-hungry photographers perma-nently banished from Las Vegas.

Traveling to my appointments wouldn't be as much of a problem, since everyone involved had been sworn to secrecy, and also, I would be coming and going at irregular intervals. It wasn't anything close to the same as being at the coffee shop from five-thirty to three-thirty every day.

And I couldn't forget what Deanne had said to me only a week earlier, during a quiet time after the early morning rush.

"You don't need to worry about me," she'd said, and I'd blinked at her.

"Worry about you about what?" I'd returned.

"About having a job if you decide to close the coffee shop," she'd replied. "Mike's pretty sure he can get me a job with the city." As she'd paused there, her blue eyes had glinted in amusement. "I know the hours would be better."

I'd just shaken my head and told her I had no intention of closing Levitation Latte. Yes, it would be shuttered during the three days leading up to the wedding and the two weeks that followed, since Max and I would be going to Italy for our honeymoon, but I'd never planned for things to be anything except business as usual after I got back.

Now, though...now I just wasn't sure. I didn't have such a puffed-up sense of my own importance that I didn't believe Las Vegas would soldier on just fine without the coffee shop downtown, but it was something of an institution, since it had been my grandmother's business before she passed it on to me. And although she'd never come right out and said so, I knew Deanne really didn't have any interest in running it on her own.

"Let me think about it," I said at length, which was about all I could offer Max right then.

Because he knew me, he didn't try to press the issue, only gave my waist another reassuring squeeze before he let go so he could reach for his own glass of wine.

"Absolutely," he said. "Now, let's go outside and enjoy some of this sunshine."

THE REST OF THE AFTERNOON WAS LOW-key enough. We talked about our upcoming trip to Italy and some of the minutiae of the reception... anything except the background issues I knew wouldn't go away just because we were currently ignoring them.

Well, the paparazzi problem would probably cure itself after the wedding. I wouldn't delude myself into believing the local celebrity photographers in Italy would leave us alone...there was a reason why the phrase had been coined in that language...but still, we hadn't told anyone about our itinerary, and since several large chunks of our stay would be spent in private villas in the countryside, not in hotels in major cities, we'd be fairly difficult to track down.

A little after six, though, just as the aroma of the lasagna Lou had concocted for that night's dinner was beginning to drift through the house, Max got a call from Al, who was currently watching the main gates to the ranch.

"Paps trying to storm the castle?" Max inquired, a smile quirking at one corner of his mouth.

Because the phone's volume was turned up fairly high, I could hear Al's answer clearly enough. "Nope," he said. "It's pretty quiet out here. But I have someone who says she needs to see Skye."

"'She'?" I echoed, mystified. The only person I could think of who might want to see me in person right now was Deanne...or maybe Andie Ingram, although I had to believe the caterer would have called rather than show up at the ranch to discuss the menu. Besides, Al and Lou knew Deanne almost as well as they knew me, and would have referred to her by name.

"Yeah," Al said. "Someone named Alicia. She says she's your mother."

CHAPTER 2

Uninvited Guest

"You said you were never coming back to Las Vegas," I told Alicia Petrucci, my tone flat. Next to me on the couch, Max nodded, his eyes narrowed. Although he personally hadn't had any negative interactions with Alicia, he knew how much her previous visit to my hometown had upset me and therefore didn't have any reason to think good thoughts about her.

"I know that," Alicia replied, looking unperturbed. Just like the last time I'd seen her, she was dressed simply but impeccably, this time in a black wrap dress and black boots with kitten heels. Plain silver hoops hung from her ears, and a wide silver cuff bracelet was her only other ornament. "But circumstances have changed."

"'Changed' how?" Max asked, voice sharpening.

She didn't reply at first. Her hands knotted themselves on her knee, and she stared down at them in silence for a moment. Then she smiled a little. "You two have been in the news a lot."

"So?" Max returned, still with that hard note in his tone which wasn't at all like him. "Just the price of doing business when you're a celebrity."

The faint lift at the corner of Alicia's mouth didn't fade. Although her appearance wasn't quite as much of a shock as it had been when she first turned up on my doorstep a year earlier, it was still strange to see so much of myself in her face, in the big dark eyes and dark arched brows, the slightly long nose and full mouth. Pretty much the only true O'Malley traits I'd inherited had been the ones no one could see—namely, being able to read the truth in tea leaves and sometimes viewing the future...or the past...in my dreams.

"It may be the price of business," she said mildly, "but the true cost is that anyone will then know about your personal affairs. The elder Petrucci witches may not camp out on TMZ, but even they occasionally see the cover of *People* magazine when they're standing in line at the grocery store."

Oh, hell. *Hell.*

Maybe if Alicia hadn't divorced herself from my life this last time just as precipitously as she'd done when I was a baby, I might have stopped to think that Max's and my engagement being so public was even less fun than I'd first believed. But with Alicia out of sight and out of mind, and with being so wrapped up in the engagement and preparations for our wedding, I simply hadn't realized that unfriendly eyes way over on the other side of the country might see the news about Max's engagement and figure out that Alicia had been doing some major-league deception of her own, considering how much we looked alike and how they knew she'd passed through Las Vegas some thirty years earlier, even though of course she'd managed to conceal the teeny, tiny fact that she'd left behind a husband and child when she returned to New York.

In her own mind, it probably hadn't been deception at all, of course. No, she'd most likely told herself she was protecting me, doing her best to keep the elder witches in her family from learning that she had another daughter in addition to the daughter and son she'd had with the husband who'd died a year earlier...the husband those elders had chosen for her.

Something inside me seemed to sink, but I told myself I shouldn't borrow trouble, that there could be a perfectly logical reason why Alicia Petrucci had shown up now, just a scant ten days before my marriage to Max Sullivan.

"You see where this is going," she said, and now her expression turned sad.

I couldn't even nod. On the couch next to me, Max shifted uneasily, appearing to sense both our vibes, even if he couldn't quite put a finger on what was wrong.

"They're very angry with me, my aunts," she said, and my paralysis lifted enough for me to blink.

"Your *aunts?*" I blurted.

Alicia inclined her head ever so slightly. "Yes, my mother passed away some years ago, but her sisters are still in charge of the family."

"You never told me the elders were my great-aunts," I managed to say. My head was swimming, and if it hadn't been for Max's solid presence there on the sofa next to me, I wondered if I might have passed out then and there.

At least she didn't say, *You never asked.* Her mouth twitched a little, and she replied, "Because I was doing my best to keep you away from the Petruccis, I didn't see the point in telling you. As far as I was concerned, the less you knew, the better. But yes, Isabella, Carmela, and Vittoria run things in the Petrucci family—or at least, they do now that your grandmother is dead. Anyway, what matters now is that they know you exist, and since you are the eldest of my daughters, they want to make sure you assume the powers and responsibilities that have been yours since birth."

I really didn't like the sound of that. Almost by its own volition, my hand crept toward Max, and he took it and wrapped his fingers around mine, warm and strong and real.

With Max holding me, I had to be safe... didn't I?

A slight shift in Alicia's gaze told me she'd noticed the gesture. Sad expression returning, she said, "And that means you must also follow the family tradition, and marry the man they decree."

At once, Max's fingers clamped down on mine. I didn't protest, though, was glad to see his reaction was so instant, so emphatic.

"Not a chance in hell," he snapped. "What is this, the Dark Ages? Skye is marrying the man she chose, which is me."

Alicia let out a small huff of a breath, almost but not quite amused. "I'm afraid that won't be up to you."

"Oh, yes, it will," I said firmly. The pressure of Max's fingers on mine seemed to have given me the necessary courage to add, "Like Max said, this isn't the Dark Ages. I'm engaged to the man I love, and if you think my great-aunts are going to come stick their noses in my business, then you've got another thing coming. Max and I are getting married on the twenty-seventh, and that's the end of it."

Her mouth curved. "Oh, no," she said. "I'm afraid it's only the beginning."

She didn't ask us to see her out. Good thing, because as soon as the front door shut behind her, Max practically launched himself from the sofa. "Just who the hell does she think she is?"

"A woman who's used to doing what she's told," I replied, and rose as well so I could stand next to him. "But I can kind of understand why."

Max stared down at me with disbelieving blue eyes. "You think she's right?"

"Of course not," I said at once, and reached over to take both his hands in mine. "That's not what I'm saying at all. But look at it this way— she was raised to believe it was her duty to do what her family expected of her. That road trip when she met my father and married him? It was just a little blip on the radar. After she abandoned us, she went back to New York and did exactly what the elders told her to do, which was to marry the man they wanted her to marry and have a couple of kids with him. Her whole life, she's been brainwashed into thinking she had to be a good little robot...and brood mare...for the Petrucci family."

Although he didn't quite relax, something in

Max's posture seemed to ease up a bit. "Whereas you were raised to think for yourself."

"Exactly," I said. "I don't have a problem with telling them no, but...."

"But?"

"I'm really not sure how they're going to react," I responded. "I mean, they're the elder witches in a family that's been passing down magic for generations. You've seen the little bit I can do with the magic from the Petrucci side of me, and it's scary enough on its own. I have to believe they have powers we can't begin to imagine."

"Well, that's reassuring." However, he didn't let go of my hands, but only tightened his grip on them, as if he feared the Petrucci witches were going to appear right in front of us and physically whisk me away. "How are we supposed to fight people like that?"

"I don't know," I said. "It's not like I have any experience with this kind of thing."

Max released a breath, but before he could reply, Lou called from the kitchen, "Dinner!"

Talk about timing.

My fiancé must have been thinking about the same thing. However, since he also knew that Lou was not a fan of people who delayed sitting down to dinner and letting the food he'd worked so hard to prepare get cold, he just said, "Guess we'd better eat."

The two of us headed into the dining room, and did our best to appear enthusiastic about the lasagna Lou set down in front of us a few minutes later. To be fair, the food smelled amazing, and I told myself I needed to eat despite my unsettled stomach.

A few sips of Montepulciano and a couple of bites of lasagna did make me feel a lot better, though. Next to me at the head of the table, Max appeared similarly revived by the food. After taking a swallow of wine, he said, "Well, this has definitely improved my outlook on life."

"Maybe the solution is right in front of us," I joked, trying my best to put a lighter spin on the situation. "All we have to do is invite my great-aunts over for dinner and ply them with a Sicilian feast courtesy of Lou, and all our problems will be solved."

Max chuckled, but I could tell he'd forced the laugh because he wanted to make me feel better, and not because he thought my suggestion would really fix the mess we'd found ourselves in. "Follow it up with some of your tiramisu," he said, "and you might just have the answer."

I smiled at him, but could feel the smile fading almost as soon as it touched my lips. "But really, what are we supposed to do if these supposed great-aunts of mine just show up and tell me I have to marry some random guy?"

"We fight it," Max said, tone at the same time unworried but also firm enough that I knew he didn't intend to back down...ever. "For one thing, forcing someone into marriage has to be some kind of trafficking. We can let Chief DeVargas know what's going on, and she can send these Petrucci witches right back to New York or straight to jail. I really don't care which."

It must be nice to be so confident all the time. Problem was, while I knew that Max generally was very good at getting his own way...politely, not by doing anything that would hurt people or step on them...we weren't dealing with recalcitrant producers or demanding directors.

No, we were dealing with a bunch of witches from a family that had been practicing magic for literally centuries.

"Well, we can try that," I said, doing my best to be diplomatic. He appeared convinced that we'd be able to get the authorities to step in and handle all this legally, and I didn't want to completely shoot him down. "But I think we also need to prepare ourselves for the possibility that they're going to fight dirty."

Max looked as though he was about to take another bite of lasagna, but after my comment, he set down his fork, mouth twisting. "Well, we can fight dirty back. I'll get a restraining order or something."

"You think a restraining order is going to stop a group of powerful witches?" I returned, and his shoulders lifted.

"Well, it might slow them down a little," he said. "I mean, the cops tend to take restraining orders that protect celebrities more seriously."

There was no bravado in his voice as he made that comment, only a simple statement of fact. And while I didn't like the idea of famous people getting preferential treatment, I really couldn't argue with what he'd said. It was just a sad part of reality.

"But don't you need to have evidence of threats being made against you before you can even file for a restraining order?" I asked next. "Right now, all we have is Alicia's word that the Petrucci elders want me to marry someone they've chosen."

It still felt a little weird to refer to my mother by her first name, but since she'd never been a part of my life—well, except for deciding to appear at inopportune times so she could stir up trouble—I definitely wasn't going to call her "Mom."

A second or two passed while Max appeared to consider my words. "I guess you do," he said, disappointment clear in his tone. "But you don't think she was telling the truth?"

I wished I could answer yes. Unfortunately, I knew Alicia wouldn't have come back to Las Vegas unless she had a very good reason—in this case, to warn me about what my great-aunts were plotting.

"Oh, I think she was," I said, and reached for my glass of Montepulciano. "I'm just not sure what we're supposed to do about any of it."

THAT NIGHT, MAX SLEPT PEACEFULLY NEXT to me, but slumber didn't seem to be in the cards for me...at least, not any time soon. No, my brain kept churning, trying to come up with a way to get us out of this predicament.

What if we eloped? Deanne would be disappointed, of course, but once I explained why we'd done such a thing, she'd understand. And running away to get married would also ensure that the paparazzi wouldn't get any of the wedding shots they so desperately wanted. We would have wasted a lot of money, since it was way too late in the game to get any of our deposits back...not that I thought Max would care a bit about any of that.

And while I'd always dreamed of an intimate, elegant wedding here in my hometown, better to present the Petrucci witches with a *fait accompli* than to have them prevent me from marrying the man I loved.

I reached over and touched him on the shoulder. "Max."

His eyes flared open at once. Although he slept like the dead, he also had the unique ability to awake immediately and not be groggy at all, something he'd probably cultivated over the years to cope with sleeping in strange places and having odd schedules while on film shoots. "What's the matter?"

"Nothing's wrong," I assured him. "It's just that I figured it out. What if we elope tomorrow?"

He sat up. The covers slipped down, revealing his gorgeously muscled shoulders and chest, but I didn't have time to be distracted by his physique. "'Elope'?" he repeated, sounding as if he'd never heard the word before.

"Yes," I said. "I can get up like I'm going to work, but instead of heading into town, we can go to the airport just down the road. We can fly out of there and then get a connecting flight in Denver or Phoenix, and be out of the country before the Petruccis have any idea about what's going on."

His head tilted to one side as he appeared to consider my suggestion. "You won't miss having a big wedding?"

"No," I said stoutly, even though I knew that was a little bit of a lie. "The important thing is for us to be married, right?"

"It is," he agreed, and even in the dimness of the bedroom we shared, I could see the glint in his eyes. "And eloping is a great idea. Good thing I bought that plane."

That was for sure. He'd been taking flying lessons for months now, and back at the end of February, had bought himself a pretty little four-seat Cessna, one of the company's higher-end offerings but still something a lot easier to manage than a private jet. It wouldn't get us to Rome, obviously, but it was definitely big enough to fly us to Denver, which was only a little more than three hundred miles away. From there, we could easily get out of the country...and far away from the clutches of my scheming great-aunts.

"Is it ready to fly?" I asked. Sure, I'd come up with what felt like a good plan, but if we got slowed down by having to refuel, it might put our stealthy getaway in jeopardy.

Now Max smiled, his teeth flashing in the darkness. "She is. I fueled her up the day before yesterday, since I figured I'd get some flying in before things with the wedding got too crazy."

And now they were getting even crazier. Still, I couldn't think of a better way to slip out of Las Vegas without anyone noticing. Once we were safely in the air, I'd text Deanne and let her know I wouldn't be opening the shop tomorrow after all, although I wouldn't give the reason why. I knew I was hoping she wouldn't ask too many questions, considering we'd discussed that very topic only a few days ago. No, I was crossing my fingers and praying she'd only think I'd changed my mind at the last minute.

There was still a lot of business that would be left hanging, but we could handle all that once we were in Rome. I had to believe the Petrucci elders would be royally pissed off, and yet, once Max and I were safely married, how much could they really do?

"Then it's a plan," I said, and paused. "Or... is it?"

"It's a great plan," Max replied at once, and leaned over to kiss me. "You're brilliant *and* beautiful, Skye. Now, let's get to sleep—we have a big day ahead."

That was for sure. With any luck, we'd be sleeping in Rome tomorrow night.

I lay down and snuggled against Max, and this time, I fell right asleep.

Only to be awakened by my alarm clock going off at four-thirty, but I'd been expecting that. We bounced out of bed and headed for the bathroom, which luckily had a huge shower that could accommodate both of us at the same time.

Too bad we couldn't indulge in any fun while

we were in that shower, but I knew time was of the essence. Technically, the general aviation airport near the ranch ran on a dawn-to-dusk schedule and it would still be dark when we got there, meaning we really shouldn't take off until around six. However, I knew Max wasn't going to worry about such niceties and was willing to get his hand slapped by the FAA if it meant we were able to escape Las Vegas under cover of darkness.

I hadn't really been planning to pack like this, but at least I already had a rough idea of which clothes I'd meant to take on our Roman honeymoon. Because I knew time was of the essence, though, I only brought my weekender bag and one rolling suitcase, and not the three or four bags I'd intended for the trip.

Well, I told myself as I zipped up the weekender bag, *you can just go shopping in Rome for any bits and pieces you need. I'm sure Max won't mind.*

That was for sure. He loved buying me things, and would probably be all too willing to load me up with designer clothes.

It seemed as though Max had similar plans in mind, since he only had one suitcase, a large weekender slightly bigger than mine.

When we got to the kitchen, it was to find Lou already there, brewing a pot of coffee. He lifted an inquiring eye at the two of us and our luggage, and said, "Going somewhere?"

"Yep," Max said easily. "We decided to go on a little trip. Mind running interference through the front gate? Just make it look like you're taking Skye to work."

"No problem," Lou replied, although I saw him send a wistful glance at the coffeemaker, as though he wished he could wait to have a few sips before he got on the road.

Max must have picked up on his bodyguard's thoughts, because he grinned and said, "The coffee'll still be here when you get back."

"True."

Without saying another word, Lou headed out front where his 4Runner was parked. After we watched his headlights move away from the house and down the gravel lane that led to the main road, we headed into the garage, put our luggage in the storage compartment of Max's Bronco, and slowly backed out.

Although I'd come and gone along this back route from the ranch numerous times, I'd never done it at o'dark thirty like this. Max drove a little more slowly than usual, obviously doing his best to avoid the biggest bumps and holes. Still, there were a few times when we hit something so hard, I feared we were going to blow a tire.

But then the Bronco would soldier on, and when we reached the road, I released a breath.

Almost there.

The airport's access road was guarded by a gate with a key card lock. Max had his card ready, and a moment later, we were headed toward the area off to one side where he kept his plane parked. He actually had hangar space, but when the weather was nice and he was flying several times a week, he didn't bother to put the plane back inside.

However, the empty hangar provided an excellent spot to park the Bronco where it wouldn't be seen. He turned off the engine, and the two of us jumped out of the SUV and grabbed our luggage, then headed toward his Cessna.

As we got closer to the little plane, my footsteps slowed.

No, that wasn't possible.

Three women stood there, all of them wearing black. The tallest one, who had silver hair that gleamed an odd, pale orange under the sodium-vapor lights at the airport, sent me a chilling smile.

"Hello, Skye," she said. "Going somewhere?"

CHAPTER 3

Witches Three

Adrenaline flooded through me and my first impulse was to run, but I knew that wouldn't do any good. If the Petrucci witches had been able to figure out exactly what Max and I were up to, then there didn't seem to be any hope of escape.

They'd find me no matter what I did, how fast I ran.

Max, on the other hand, didn't seem cowed at all. "Yes, we are going somewhere, actually," he said, chin up. "And since you're blocking the cockpit door, I'll ask you to kindly step aside."

The three witches exchanged amused glances. "Oh, I don't think so," the woman with the pale hair said. "You may be an action hero on the silver screen, but there isn't much you can do here."

"That a fact?" he returned, hands on his hips. I

got the feeling he wished this really was one of his movies, because then his hands would have been resting on a pair of pistols. However, although the ranch had a gun safe loaded with a couple of rifles and a shotgun—more for keeping mountain lions and coyotes away from the horses than to defend against human predators—Max obviously hadn't brought any weapons with him on this trip.

"It is," the woman said, sounding more amused than anything else. "And now I think we should all go back to your ranch so we can discuss this like civilized people."

"'Civilized'?" I echoed, not bothering to hide the scorn in my voice. "What's civilized about forcing someone to marry a person they don't even know?"

"I think you'll have a different opinion on the matter when you see who we've chosen for you," the Petrucci witch replied, obviously unperturbed. "But come—there is a much more comfortable place to have this conversation." She turned toward the witch who stood on her left side, a woman with wild, curly black hair shot through with gray. "Vittoria, if you would?"

"Of course," the other woman said.

Maybe she murmured something under her breath, or maybe her magic didn't even need that kind of focus. All I knew was that one moment I was standing on the tarmac at the airport, and the next, I was sitting on one of the leather couches in the living room at the ranch. The big coffee table had five cups on it, all of which emitted a fragrant steam.

"It was good of your bodyguard to make the coffee," the silver-haired witch said as she reached for the cup in front of her. "It smells wonderful."

Next to me, Max was rigid with shock. Yes, he'd seen me perform small bits of magic here and there, but I really hadn't done much with my Petrucci powers, and I guessed he honestly hadn't stopped to contemplate what the witches on that side of the family might be able to do with magic they'd been using all their lives.

Then he found his voice, demanding, "What the *hell?*"

The curly-haired witch smiled. "It just seemed easier to come here via magical means than to wait for you to drive back in the dark. Also, this way, there wasn't any chance of you trying to escape again."

That was for sure. I spoke then, sounding a lot steadier than I'd thought I would, considering the circumstances. "You can use all the magic tricks you want," I said. "But Max and I are getting married, no matter what you do."

Another quick exchange of glances. Then the third witch, the one who hadn't spoken yet, sent me an indulgent smile. She appeared to be the middle sister, although her long black hair didn't have a single streak of silver, and her face also didn't show many signs of age, except a couple of lines around her clear gray eyes and a single, stubborn one in the middle of her brows.

Did witches have some kind of anti-aging secret? If these three women were my great-aunts, then they had to be in their seventies. However, they looked twenty years younger than that, maybe more.

Then again, my mother didn't look her age, either. If you stood the two of us side by side, a lot of people probably would think she was my older sister.

"We know that you've loved Max for a very long time," the witch with the gray eyes said, and I sent her a piercing look.

"How would you know that?" I demanded. "You didn't even know I existed until a little while ago."

Her mouth curved again in a smile I found extremely unpleasant in its condescension. "Because that piece in *People* magazine said so."

All right, I had made the somewhat embarrassing confession that I'd had a crush on Max for most of my life. At the time, I hadn't seen any reason to hide that piece of information, and besides, I'd thought it might be somewhat relatable to the magazine's readers. After all, most people could relate to a childhood crush, even if those feelings were rarely reciprocated.

"Okay, fine," I said, knowing I couldn't really argue the truth of something that had been printed in black and white for all the world to see. "And you're right. I've loved Max forever, and I'm going to go on loving him. Nothing you say is going to change any of that."

"Love him or not, you will not be marrying him," the silver-haired witch said. "You must understand, Skye, that being a Petrucci witch means you have certain obligations."

"Obligations my mother wanted me to avoid," I replied. "That's why she hid me from you—she wanted me to be able to live my own life."

The curly-haired witch—Vittoria—frowned. "Alicia made a huge mistake in trying to keep your existence a secret. That is not how the Petrucci family handles such things. And that is why we're here now, to rectify her mistake."

"My sister is correct," the witch with the silver hair said. "The reason why our powers have remained strong throughout the generations is that we've been very careful about who we married, who we had children with."

Next to me, Max stiffened, and I got the feeling he wanted to take me by the hand and stalk out of the room...and knew that doing so would be futile, since Vittoria could just blip us back here whenever she wanted. "Sounds like you're running a breeding program, not having a family," he retorted.

"Call it what you want," the silver-haired witch said, her tone almost too mild. Then she smiled again, adding, "I suppose I should introduce the three of us. I am Isabella Petrucci, and this is Carmela"—she nodded toward the witch with the gray eyes—"and Vittoria is our youngest sister."

"Did someone arrange all your marriages?" I asked sourly.

Although I'd hoped those words would throw Isabella off-balance, she didn't seem too bothered by my question. "Of course," she said without a single blink. "The witches who were the family elders when we were young made that determination, and we've all been very happy."

"Do your husbands know about this little field trip to Las Vegas to coerce your great-niece into an arranged marriage?" Max cut in, and this time, all three of the witches assumed a matching set of Mona Lisa smiles.

Carmela was the one who replied. "Our husbands, I am sorry to say, are no longer with us. However, even if we weren't widows, the men in the Petrucci family know it is not their place to question the actions of their elders."

I reflected that the mortality rate of Petrucci husbands seemed awfully high, especially when you considered that my mother's husband had passed away only a year or so ago as well. Was there some kind of black widow vibe going on here, or was it simply that my great-aunts really were a good deal older than they appeared?

"At any rate," Vittoria said, "we simply cannot have a Petrucci witch choosing her own spouse. It will dilute the blood."

Max's eyebrow went up, and I hastily remarked, "If your magic really only passes through the female line, like my mother described, then what difference does it make who a witch marries? The guy doesn't have anything to do with it."

"Oh, that's where you're wrong," Isabella said. "Every once in a great while, we may consider allowing an outsider to marry a Petrucci, just to keep the bloodlines from getting too interconnected, but in general, we marry cousins distant enough that we don't have to worry about inbreeding. That way, the men still carry the magic of the Petruccis within them, even if they can't use that magic themselves."

This was getting better and better. Now I was supposed to marry a cousin in addition to ditching Max?

"Well, I don't care what your traditions were, or are," I declared. "I'm not marrying a cousin. I'm marrying Max. And I think you'd better leave."

Max took my hand, and through some

unspoken agreement, we both got to our feet. "Skye's right," he said. "You really should leave."

The three sisters shared another glance, this one obviously amused. "Oh, we'll be leaving," Vittoria commented. "But so will Skye."

And again there was one of those abrupt shifts in scene, with the Petrucci elders and me vanishing from the living room at the ranch and appearing in another space that was equally familiar, even though I hadn't been here for a while.

The kitchen in my childhood home, miles away from Max's ranch.

"What the hell are we doing here?" I demanded.

Isabella glanced around the room. Even though I'd been living with Max for the past five months, I still stopped in at the house every other week or so, just to make sure everything was okay and that the team I'd hired to come and clean once a month was doing a good job. They'd been here this week, which was why all the fixtures gleamed and there was no discernible dust anywhere.

"This is your home, isn't it?" she asked.

"I own it, if that's what you mean," I replied, not sure how I was supposed to respond. Yes, the house was still mine, mostly because I'd been loath to put it up for sale even though I knew I would never live here again, that the ranch was now my forever home.

"Some separation from Max is a good thing," Carmela put in. "You will stay here until you are married to Christian."

Which meant I'd be living in the old farmhouse until hell froze over, since I certainly wasn't marrying anyone except Max. "I told you—I'm not marrying this Christian person," I snapped.

"You say that now," Isabella responded, her tone far too unruffled. "I think you will change your mind soon enough."

Fat chance, I thought. However, since it seemed like we were the irresistible force meeting the immovable object, I decided to try another tack. "And how am I supposed to explain all this?" I asked. "Everyone in town—hell, everyone in the *world* who's been paying attention to the story— knows I've been living with Max for all these months. What do I tell people who ask why I'm suddenly back at my own house?"

"That's easy enough," Carmela said. "You simply say that you want the wedding to be old-fashioned, and you want to have Max carry you over the threshold at the ranch after you're married. That it would feel odd for you to have been living with him when that happens, so you're going to be in your old house for now."

Anyone who knew me at all wouldn't believe that story for a second. I almost pointed that out, then realized Carmela—and her two sisters—really didn't care what people thought. They just wanted me to stay put so I was safely away from Max and in a position where I could be wooed by this Christian person.

If he even had any intention of wooing me. After all, you could say I was kind of a sure thing. The elders had decreed that he was to be my husband, so there wasn't much point in bringing me flowers or taking me out for romantic dinners.

Not that I had any intention of letting him do a single one of those things. Maybe the Petrucci elders could keep me trapped in this house, but they couldn't force me to have any real interactions with the man.

...could they?

"You've overlooked one important thing," I countered. "I've had the paparazzi chasing me for the past five months. When I stayed at Max's house, I had Lou and Al and Max looking after me and making sure the photographers didn't get too close. What am I supposed to do about that if I'm living here by myself?"

Any hopes I might have flummoxed the witches with that question were immediately dashed by Isabella's answering smile. "That's not a problem at all," she said. "I'll simply cast a spell to keep them at least a hundred feet away from you, no matter where you are or what you're doing.

That way, you'll be able to drive to work safely, and come and go as you please."

While it normally would have been reassuring to know I wouldn't have to worry about tripping over a paparazzo while running across town to Walmart to stock up on laundry soap, I couldn't quite ignore the implications of her words. "So... you expect me to go to work during all this?"

Carmela nodded. "It's very important for everything to seem normal for you, and that means continuing to run your coffee shop as you have all these months. Isabella's spell will protect you, and when you break off your engagement to Max, it will only seem like you've had a change of heart."

"After all, who could blame you?" Vittoria added. Her black eyes sparkled with what I thought was mischief...or maybe simple satisfaction that she and her sisters had been able to block me at every turn. "It has to have been exhausting, avoiding photographers all these months, never knowing when a story about you and Max might show up in the *National Enquirer* or on TMZ. You can tell everyone that, while you love Max, you need a quieter life than that."

I listened to all those supposedly reasonable words in growing horror. Much of what she was saying would seem all too plausible to anyone who didn't know me very well, who didn't know that

I'd put up with pretty much anything in order to be with Max Sullivan.

Still, I wasn't about to let myself be completely steamrollered.

"Even if anyone believes that cock-and-bull story," I retorted, "and I'm not saying they will, how am I supposed to explain taking up with a completely different guy less than two weeks before my wedding?"

"You don't have to explain anything," Isabella said. Her expression was so serene, you would have thought we were discussing the next day's weather, and not how I was supposed to break off my engagement to the only man I could ever love and marry some rando they'd chosen for me. "You can see Christian quietly, get to know him better. And you'll be married in New York and start a new life there. No one here in Las Vegas has to know anything about it. You can say you needed to leave New Mexico because there were too many uncomfortable memories here for you."

They had it all figured out, didn't they?

Well, except the part where I'd refuse to have anything to do with this Christian Petrucci. The elders could send him over, but that didn't mean I had to talk to him or interact with him in any meaningful way.

Still, I knew they had me boxed in. I could lock myself in the bathroom and refuse to come out, but I was pretty sure witches who were capable of teleporting themselves and others from one spot to another—and who somehow had known exactly where Max and I would be this morning, even though we obviously hadn't announced our plans to anyone—wouldn't have any trouble unlocking a door. And, as they'd already proven today, I had absolutely no chance of escape.

"And you really don't need to worry about Max," Carmela said in response to my stony silence that followed Isabella's last pronouncement. "He's a handsome, rich, extremely successful man. It's not as if we're condemning him to a life alone. He'll forget about you soon enough."

Those terrible words made me wish I had powers equal to their own. That way, I could throw a fireball in Isabella's direction, or envelop the three sisters in a sticky web that would allow me to escape.

You do *have powers,* I told myself. *You just don't know how to use them.*

But I needed to learn...fast.

"Max will never forget me," I shot back. "You're just a bunch of deluded hags who never got to experience true love because your husbands were forced on you. But Max and I love each other—and real love like ours never gives up."

Isabella's eyes narrowed at the word "hags,"

while Carmela's and Vittoria's cheeks burned with angry color.

Good. I wanted to upset them even a tenth as much as they'd upset me.

A thought leaped into my brain. One thing about Petrucci magic—it wasn't about reciting spells or brewing potions, but simply willing the power within me to do what I wanted it to do. I'd avoided using it because it was too big and too scary, but right now, I couldn't think of anything scarier than being torn from Max before we'd even had a chance to start our life together.

The doors to all the lower kitchen cupboards sprang open, and pots and pans and the heavy cast-iron baking sheets I preferred for making croissants flew through the air, converging on the elders. Immediately, they flung up their hands to shield themselves—but not before my favorite eight-inch cast-iron pan smacked Carmela on the side of her head.

She let out a frightened yelp, and immediately Isabella cried out, "Enough!"

At once, all the pots and pans and baking sheets fell to the floor, the clang of their impact muffled a bit by the wooden surface. Good thing I'd decided against tile when I remodeled the room.

"Impressive," Isabella went on, as Carmela rubbed her head and Vittoria stared down at the quiescent pieces of bakeware on the floor, as though she wasn't sure whether they were about to come to life once again and begin a second assault. "But, as you can see, ultimately fruitless. You have the Petrucci power within you, and that's good. However, you're not trained...and even if you were, your powers still wouldn't be a match for the ones we've been honing for decades." She stopped there, her gaze moving almost ostentatiously to the clock on the stove. "But you're already late for work. You need to go—and you need to make sure you say nothing of this to anyone. Otherwise, it won't go well for your precious Max."

Impotent fury churned in me, because I knew her threat was impossible to ignore. All the same, I opened my mouth, hoping I could come up with some kind of halfway coherent protest...

...only to have the scene change again. Now I stood in the kitchen at the shop, alone. The big clock I'd hung on one wall to make sure I kept an accurate count of the time ticked away, telling me I only had a few minutes before Deanne showed up.

God, Deanne. What in the world was I supposed to tell her?

Not a damn thing, I told myself. I couldn't forget Isabella's threat, couldn't forget how she and her sisters had powers that warped space, if not time, and that there didn't seem to be much they weren't capable of. If I told Deanne my tale of woe and the Petrucci witches somehow found out, what was to prevent them from making sure Max suffered some kind of terrible accident?

I couldn't risk that. They might have separated the two of us for now, but I'd figure out how to outsmart them.

Maybe.

In the meantime, I knew I had to do whatever I could to keep Max safe.

CHAPTER 4

The New Normal

I couldn't help looking at my phone after Carmela teleported me from my house to the coffee shop, even though I knew I was hideously late getting started with that morning's batches of muffins and coffee.

Ten separate texts from Max, all of them variations on, *Are you okay? Where are you?*

Replying would delay me that much more, but I didn't care.

I'm okay. I'm at the shop. They're forcing me to stay at my house and away from you, but they want me to try to act natural otherwise and keep coming to work.

Almost immediately, he sent back.

I'm coming over.

Oh, hell. While I would have liked nothing more than to have Max with me right now, to feel the reassurance of his embrace and see his bright, encouraging smile, I knew having him at the coffee shop would be inviting disaster.

I don't think that's a good idea. The three witches made it pretty clear they're keeping an eye on me, and that they want us to stay away from each other. They didn't exactly threaten you, but we can't take the risk.

No immediate response to that one. I forced myself to go out front and get a batch of coffee started, phone sitting on the counter while I worked.

Then,

You're sure about this?

I set down the carafe of filtered water I was holding so I could reply right away.

I'm sure I don't want you to get hurt. Just hang in there while I try to figure this out. Please?

This time, he answered immediately.

All right. I don't like it...but you know better than I do what those women are capable of.

Did I, though? Okay, I'd seen them stop my assault with the pots and pans before it barely got started, so I knew their powers were much, much stronger than mine. And I had to believe they'd be utterly ruthless about achieving their goals. Otherwise, they wouldn't have come to Las Vegas in the first place.

I don't like it, either. Just trust me and stay away so you don't attract any attention.

All right...love you, Skye.

Love you, Max.

In that moment, I thought I loved him more than I ever had. He was trusting me to figure this out, wasn't ignoring my request and charging in anyway, consequences be damned.

Our convo over, I slipped my phone into my apron pocket and hurried into the back of the shop so I could start mixing up a batch of muffins. Less than five minutes later, Deanne appeared. She sent a startled glance at the big bowl of batter in front of me; at this hour, those muffins should have already been in the oven and almost done.

"Everything okay?" she asked.

Everything was pretty much as not okay as it could be, but this was one time I didn't dare confide in my best friend, not when I didn't know what the Petrucci witches might do if I started spreading my tale of woe to anyone, even Deanne.

"Oh, it's fine," I replied, praying that I sounded breezy and completely unconcerned about my late start. "I forgot to turn on the alarm on my phone last night." I paused there, wondering if I should say anything else. However, I knew Deanne would figure out sooner rather than later that I wasn't staying at Max's ranch, so I realized I might as well forge ahead and tell her I was staying at my old house for the next week. "I'm back at the house until the wedding."

Her big blue eyes opened even wider in surprise. As usual when she came to work, she had her bright blonde hair pulled back in a ponytail, although, since we really didn't have a dress code at Levitation Latte, she was wearing a cheerful green T-shirt and jeans. "Oh, my God. Did you and Max have a fight?"

"No, of course not," I snapped, glad that at least my indignation sounded genuine. "I just thought it would be more romantic to meet at the church when we didn't just spend the night before together. This way, it feels more old-fashioned, more traditional."

One of her eyebrows arched, and she gave me a very direct look. I picked up the basket of fresh blueberries that had been sitting off to one side and poured them into the batter, slowly folding the fruit into the mixture, all the while hoping my friend couldn't see the lie in my expression.

It seemed my desperation must have made me a decent actress, because after a long pause, she said, "Okay. It sounds a little weird to me, but if Max is on board with it—"

"Oh, he is," I replied. "He's really looking forward to carrying me over the threshold."

Well, at least that comment wasn't a lie.

Deanne shrugged. "You do you. Need any help with those muffins?"

The cavalry had come to the rescue. She might not have completely understood why Max and I wanted to spend this last week living apart, but now it seemed she only wanted to give me any assistance she could.

"Yes, please," I said gratefully. "Can you pour the batter into the tin so I can start mixing up the apricot cashew muffins?"

She nodded, and took over at my station while I hurried to the shelf where I kept all my dry ingredients. Something about her expression was still questioning, but I knew she wouldn't pry.

Thank God.

Now all I had to do was survive today...and hope some miraculous solution to my witch problem would present itself before everything went to hell.

UNFORTUNATELY, I WASN'T STRUCK BY ANY flashes of inspiration. Because it was a Friday, the coffee shop was fairly busy, and keeping the coffee going and throwing in a second batch of blueberry muffins and one of croissants prevented me from brooding on my problems too much. Every time the door opened, I stiffened, wondering if the newcomer was Christian Petrucci coming in to introduce himself, but apparently he—or the elders —had decided that was an introduction which should take place in private. It wasn't as though Gordon would have stopped Christian from coming in, since even the paparazzi were allowed entry as long as they behaved themselves.

With everything that had been going on, I'd completely forgotten I had an appointment with Andie Ingram to walk over to the Ilfeld Ballroom and do a final survey of the reception arrangements. She came into the coffee shop right at three as we'd agreed, expression as bright and cheerful as the copper-red hair she always wore in a set of braids pinned up on top of her head, milkmaid style.

"Oh, hi, Andie," I said, trying not to sound too startled by her sudden appearance.

She didn't seem to notice anything was wrong, and only smiled in reply and said, "Hi, Skye. Ready to take a look at the ballroom?"

"Sure," I responded, and glanced over at Deanne. "Can you keep an eye on things for a few minutes?"

"Sure," she said. "It should be pretty quiet until closing."

Well, that was the hope. There was always the chance that a group of high school kids might decide to descend on their way home from school, but Deanne should still be able to handle such an invasion without too much trouble.

I offered her a grateful thank-you, and Andie and I headed over to the hotel. Almost in a mockery of my personal troubles, the weather had continued to be mild and warmer than normal, temperatures just kissing seventy degrees, the skies serenely blue. Just a few days earlier, I'd hoped for nothing more than to have this lovely stretch of days continue until after the wedding, but right about now, I found myself thinking a late-season snowstorm would be much more in line with my current mood.

However, I knew I couldn't let Andie see that anything was troubling me. No, we just exchanged a few comments about the weather, and headed into the hotel so we could get the key to the ballroom from the woman working at the front desk. Not so long ago, a man named Pedro Montaño had held that position, but because he'd helped Leila Moreno cover up ghost hunter Calum McRae's accidental death in one of the hotel's guest rooms last fall, he was currently on probation and definitely no longer employed by the Plaza Hotel.

Key in hand, Andie and I headed down to the ballroom. Once inside, she looked around slowly, then gave a pleased nod.

"It's such a gorgeous space," she said. "I'm so

glad they restored everything rather than trying to modernize it."

I had to agree with her. The ballroom had been built around the turn of the last century, and had tall columns at either end of the space and a gorgeous ornamental plaster ceiling. The floor was the original oak, beautifully restored and perfect for dancing.

For months, I'd been envisioning what Max's and my wedding and reception would look like in the space, what kind of flowers I'd choose to adorn the tables and the little dais at one side where the ceremony would take place. Now, though, I only felt a tight, worried knot in the pit of my stomach.

What if the witches succeeded? What if I never got the chance to stand here with Max and pledge to spend the rest of my life with him?

"Is everything okay?" Andie asked, in an echo of Deanne's words from earlier that day. "You seem a little preoccupied."

I forced a smile. "Oh, I'm all right. I guess it's just starting to sink in that this is really happening."

She smiled back at me. In contrast to her flaming red hair, she had hazel eyes with interesting gold flecks in them, striking and unusual. "A lot of brides feel that way," she said. "And I know it can start to be a little overwhelming. But I've got the menu and the cake and all the catering details handled, and it seems like your friend is doing a great job of dealing with the florist and the musicians."

Well, that sort of thing was a lot easier when you were working with someone you'd known all your life—as was the case with Rachel, the florist— or people you'd known since high school, which was the case with the band. Not our friend Kyle's country-rock band...I thought that asking him to play at my wedding might have been rubbing salt in the wound, since it had taken a long time for him to accept that we were never getting back together...but a different group who were excellent at covers and would keep the good time going at the reception. It had been important to both Max and me to have as many locals involved in the event as possible, even though he probably could have hired any band he wanted.

However, having Elton John or the Rolling Stones perform at our reception might have seemed a little ostentatious, so we'd gone with the Moonshine Mavericks instead.

Andie had stepped away from me, and was taking a series of photos with her iPhone. She'd done the same thing when we'd walked the space a few months earlier, but I could tell she was trying to refresh her memory, to make sure that all her calculations for tables and chairs were still correct.

When she was done, she came back over to me,

sliding her phone into the huge bag of multicolored patches of what looked like sari fabric that hung over one shoulder. "That should do it," she told me. "I just want to check on a few things with Deanne, and then I can head back to Santa Fe."

It seemed like an awfully long drive to only spend half an hour here, but this was a job Andie had clearly wanted to handle in person, so I didn't question her judgment. "Sure," I said. "She'll still be at the shop for a few more minutes."

We dropped off the ballroom key and walked back down to Levitation Latte. As we went, I couldn't help noticing how all the photographers who were loitering on the street kept a respectful distance. Under other circumstances, I could have expected to be swarmed just as soon as the paparazzi realized I didn't have Lou or Al with me, but now something seemed to be preventing them from getting too close.

Well, at least Isabella's magic is good for something, I thought sourly as Andie and I approached the coffee shop. *Too bad she can't put all those powers to better use than forcing me to marry someone I don't even know.*

As soon as we were inside, I realized that Kyle was standing by the counter, chatting with Deanne. He was in uniform, telling me he probably had taken a quick break to get an iced tea and maybe see if we had any leftover muffins. Today we didn't, just because I'd never gotten the chance to stock the pastry case as full as I would have liked, but he didn't seem too upset by that.

In fact, he appeared almost startled as he looked in Andie's and my direction, something in his expression and the way he unconsciously straightened telling me he was more impressed with her than he wanted to let on.

And distracted and worried as I was by the whole Petrucci situation, I couldn't help being amused. For months, I'd been wishing Kyle would find someone to date, but no one really seemed to be working out for him.

Now, though...now it sure seemed to me as if he'd found someone worthy of his interest.

"Hi, Kyle," I said, my tone breezy. "This is Andie Ingram, my caterer. Andie, this is Kyle Isaacs. He's a deputy here in town."

He took a couple of steps forward, closing the distance between us. Hand extended, he said, "It's very nice to meet you, Andie."

"And it's very nice to meet you, too," she returned, wearing a friendly smile. "Have you known Skye for very long?"

"Oh, we've all known each other forever," Deanne put in, looking amused, too. Like me, she knew Kyle well and had obviously noticed his sudden interest in the pretty caterer. "That's the thing about living in a small town."

"It seems nice," Andie commented. Her expression appeared almost wistful, although I had to admit I didn't know her well enough to judge for sure whether my assessment was accurate or not. "Small-town life, I mean. I grew up in Albuquerque, and that's about as not-small-town as you can get. Even Santa Fe seems pretty big in comparison to Las Vegas."

"That's where you live now?" Kyle asked, clearly wanting to make sure he remained an active participant in the conversation. "Santa Fe?"

She nodded. "Yes. It's a beautiful place, but it still can feel a little hectic."

Hmm. I knew I shouldn't be matchmaking now, not when I had much bigger things to be worried about, and yet I couldn't help hoping that maybe Andie wanted to settle down someplace where the pace of life was quieter, where she could really become a part of the community.

And that, I told myself, was just silly. The woman had just been named one of the top five chefs in all of New Mexico. Our state might have been small and out of the way, but serious foodies tended to agree that we had some of the best cuisine in the country. Andie's star was rising fast, and I didn't see why she'd want to give all that up to live in a backwater like Las Vegas.

Then again, people probably had said the same thing about Max, and yet here we were.

Not for long if you don't get this whole Christian Petrucci thing figured out, I thought next, and that knot of worry in my gut tightened a little.

Luckily, no one else seemed to notice I was a little preoccupied. Deanne and Kyle were telling Andie about their favorite places to eat in town, and she was saying she'd need to try some of them when she came next week for the wedding. That was the plan—she'd arrive on Friday and would stay at the Plaza Hotel, and that way she'd be right there when things really kicked into high gear.

Assuming, of course, I hadn't been shanghaied to New York and forced to marry a distant cousin.

Because it was closing time by that point—and because I knew Kyle and Andie could let themselves out and close the locked door behind them—I excused myself from the conversation so I could lock up. As usual, Gordon waited until the door was secured until he lifted a hand in a gesture of farewell and headed down the block where his SUV was parked. Sometimes the paparazzi in the vicinity would take his departure as a signal to rush over and try getting a couple of snaps before I closed the blinds, but today, they stayed across the street.

Of course they did. Isabella's spell was keeping them safely out of the way.

"I hope you don't mind me bailing," I told the group, who didn't show any sign of ending their conversation any time soon. "But it's been a long day."

"No worries," Deanne said. "Andie and I just need to finalize a few things."

"But I have to get going," Kyle put in, although he didn't look very happy about the prospect of having to leave the discussion and go back on patrol. "It was nice meeting you, Andie."

"Nice meeting you, too, Kyle," she replied. "I hope I'll see you at the wedding."

He gave an awkward nod, mumbled, "Sure," and headed for the door. I didn't know whether his embarrassment stemmed from her obvious desire to see him again, or whether he was still processing his feelings about me getting married to Max Sullivan. The situation was a little uncomfortable, but if nothing else, Kyle was an old friend of mine, and not inviting him to the wedding would have been even more awkward.

I was pretty much going on autopilot by then, but I realized as I began to walk out the back door that I didn't even know how I was supposed to get home. My car was still parked in Max's garage, miles away, and there weren't any witches around to do one of those *Bewitched* nose wiggles to beam me to my house.

But it seemed the Petrucci elders had thought of that, because when I opened the door—figuring I'd simply walk back to the house if no other alternatives presented themselves—there was my sky-blue Subaru Crosstrek, waiting in its usual spot behind the coffee shop.

Even I had to admit that was pretty impressive.

I hurried down the back steps and got in. Everything was exactly where I'd left it, right down to the little hanging ornament of pewter stars and turquoise beads Max had bought me at a craft fair in Plaza Park a while back. Looking at it sent a pang through me, although I did my best to reassure myself that not all was yet lost, and I had a whole week to figure out how to remove the Petrucci witches and their unreasonable demands permanently from my life.

First, though, I just wanted to get home.

It was a little before four by that point, after the time when kids would be walking home from school, but earlier than most people would have gotten off work. Thankful for the quiet trip, I pulled into the driveway and into the garage, then got out. It felt weird to be doing this after so many months at Max's place, but I tried to remind myself I'd been parking in my garage a lot longer than I'd been living with Max.

And I'd be with him again, no matter what.

I realized, however, that I really should have done some shopping on my way home. Like it or not, I was going to be stuck here for a while until I could get the Petruccis out of my hair, and even though the house was clean, the refrigerator and cupboards hadn't been stocked for months.

In the meantime, there was plain old water, and I supposed I could get myself some takeout tonight to tide me over. At least the witches hadn't told me I couldn't go out for food, only that I needed to stay away from Max.

And I was really, really glad that Tilly, the talking cat who used to stay overnight at my house from time to time, had pretty much taken up permanent residence in the room in the back of the shop, rather than coming to the ranch with me. She'd put down her little black paw over that, declaring there was no way she'd allow herself to be taken so far from the downtown she loved to roam.

"I am perfectly capable of taking care of myself," she'd said, in tones that hadn't allowed any argument. "I did it before I could talk, and I can do it now. There's no way you can make me go to that ranch."

Privately, I'd thought there were plenty of ways I could force her to relocate, most of which would have involved grabbing the cat, putting her in a cat carrier on the front seat of my car, and bodily moving her to Max's place. But because she'd been so adamant—and because I knew her pride would be wounded if I tried to assert any human power over her—I'd let the matter go.

Just as well. I had enough to deal with right

now without babysitting a talking cat on top of everything else.

I'd barely taken a sip of my water before the doorbell rang, and I froze. Sure, in the past the neighbors would drop by occasionally, or I'd get the odd school kid selling something for a fundraiser, but pretty much everyone nearby knew I'd been living with Max for months.

Which meant the person at the door probably wasn't anyone I wanted to see.

As much as I would have liked to pretend I wasn't home and hope they'd go away, I knew the solution to my problem wouldn't be quite that easy. I pulled in a breath, allowed myself another swallow of water, and then resolutely set the glass on the counter.

Unconsciously, my hands went up to smooth my hair, even though I knew I shouldn't be worried about what kind of impression I was about to make. Not that it would be terribly positive anyway—I'd only flicked on some mascara this morning as I was getting ready to leave, and the lip gloss I'd applied after lunch was now pretty much gone.

And I wore my usual uniform of a black top and jeans, although this stuff was a little nicer than my regular workday attire, just because I'd thought I would be getting on a plane and heading to Rome, not baking muffins and serving coffee.

The house sounded ominously quiet as I made my way to the front door. I didn't know what would have been worse—the way the doorbell had rung once and then gone quiet, or having someone impatiently pushing the button several more times.

My hand paused on the doorknob.

Just get it over with, I told myself.

Before I could stop to think, I turned the knob and opened the door. Standing outside on the porch was a man I'd never seen before, maybe around thirty-five, with sooty black hair and dark eyes and the kind of mysterious, suave looks that would have made him a shoo-in to play some Latin lover idol in an old black and white movie.

"Hello," the apparition said. "I'm Christian Petrucci."

CHAPTER 5
Mr. Christian

Maybe I blinked. I knew I stood there in dumbfounded silence for a moment or two, my brain trying to process what it was seeing. Never in all my worries about the man the Petrucci witches had picked out for me had I ever thought he'd be drop-dead gorgeous.

Not that it made a difference, I quickly reminded myself. Max was the only man for me, the only man I would ever love, and it didn't matter how handsome this Christian Petrucci had turned out to be.

Luckily, I was able to recover from my shock before the silence got too awful. I opened the door a little wider, forced a smile, and then said, "Hi. Come on in."

No point in introducing myself, after all—I was sure he already knew exactly who I was.

Christian stepped into the living room and stood there, manner a little awkward, as if he'd been about to sit down and then had realized he should probably wait for my invitation.

"You can sit on the sofa," I said quickly. "I'm afraid I don't have anything to offer you except water, though—it's been months since I lived here, and the cupboards are kind of bare."

"Water is fine," he replied. One corner of his mouth quirked a little, making me think he'd been about to smile but had decided maybe it wasn't the time for that yet. His voice had a kind of brisk quality that reminded me he was from New York, although he didn't have anything close to a truly identifiable accent.

Glad of the excuse to be away for a moment or two, I scurried off to the kitchen, where I got another glass out of a cupboard and filled it from the refrigerator door, then topped off my own glass. I didn't have any excuse to linger—it wasn't as if I'd gone in there to prep a charcuterie board— so I made myself go back out to the living room, where Christian was looking around with interest.

"You seem surprised," I said as I handed him the glass.

"I suppose I am," he replied, then waited as I seated myself in the chair across from him. "I guess I was expecting a house in New Mexico to be adobe or stucco or something."

"A lot of them are," I said. Maybe architecture was a strange topic for us to be exploring, but it felt a lot safer than talking about how he'd come here so we could meet before our arranged marriage. "But the older parts of Las Vegas were mostly built by people who came here to work on the railroad, and I guess they wanted their houses to look like what they were used to back east or in the Midwest. That's why there are a lot of these farmhouse-style homes in town."

"It's very nice," Christian said, all politeness, and then drank a little of the water I'd given him. He paused there, and the faint hint of a smile he'd been wearing shifted into the real thing.

It was a very handsome smile...but nowhere near as incandescent as one of Max's.

Since there didn't seem to be much point in beating around the bush any further, I asked, "Did your elders tell you that I'm already engaged and am getting married a week from tomorrow?"

His smile didn't fade all the way, but it did grow a little lopsided. "Yes, Aunt Isabella told me what was going on. I'll have to admit I wasn't too thrilled to be competing with someone like Max Sullivan."

"You're not competing," I said sternly. "It's not like I expect you to joust for my hand in marriage. I just want you to go back to your aunts and tell them it's not happening, and that they'll have to find someone else to be a part of their crazy Petrucci eugenics program."

Rather than look upset by my comment, Christian only shrugged and settled against the back of the couch. "They're your aunts, too," he pointed out.

"I've never seen them before today," I retorted. "They've never been a part of my life. So, we may have a blood connection, but they're not family."

"The blood connection is the most important thing," Christian said without missing a beat. "Why do you think our family has worked so hard to make sure those connections keep our witches powerful?"

Clearly, he'd been just as brainwashed as the rest of them.

I pushed myself against the back of my chair and crossed my arms, glaring at him. "And you don't have a problem marrying someone who has absolutely no interest in you, who's in love with someone else?"

Maybe his shoulders lifted ever so slightly. He had on an expertly tailored white shirt and a casual-looking gray blazer that I guessed had still cost a pretty penny. It wasn't the sort of thing you'd see anyone in Las Vegas wearing, not even Max, who certainly could have afforded those kinds of clothes. No, he was careful to be casual, to not show off, even though I knew he owned pairs of shoes that had cost more than the remodel on my powder room.

"It's not optimal," Christian admitted. "But I guess I'm hoping you'll be able to move beyond Max at some point. You may not want to believe me, but the huge majority of Petrucci marriages are happy ones, even if they've been arranged."

That sounded like a whole heck of a lot like self-delusion to me. There hadn't been a single thing my mother had said to me during her last visit that made it seem as if her marriage had been particularly happy. She'd done her duty to the family, and that was it.

Another thought occurred to me. After all, I had to fight this war on as many fronts as possible.

"It seems a little strange that you're not married yet," I said. "I mean, you're older than me, right? What, thirty-four, thirty-five?"

"Thirty-six," Christian replied, his tone calm. If he was at all offended by me commenting on his age, he didn't show it. "Actually, I was married before. She died in a traffic accident three years ago."

Oh, my God. Talk about sticking my foot in it. "I'm so sorry," I said quickly.

"It's all right," he said, still sounding remarkably unruffled. "You didn't know. We'd been trying to start a family, but nothing was working."

"My aunts don't have magic for that?" I asked,

now genuinely curious. After all, if they possessed the power to teleport people and cars, you'd think they'd be able to unblock a couple of temperamental ovaries...or give a man's reproductive system a little boost.

Christian reached for his glass of water and drank again. "No, the Petrucci witches aren't healers. They can affect the outside world in all kinds of ways, but their talents don't extend to fixing what might be wrong inside our bodies. Lydia and I had just started with IVF, but then...."

He didn't bother to finish the sentence.

I guessed he really didn't need to. My impression was that people didn't drive a lot in New York, so maybe the fatal accident had involved an Uber or a taxi, or maybe a terrible incident in a crosswalk. Whatever had happened, his wife had been taken from him in one of the worst ways possible.

"I'm sorry," I said again. "But I also think it's pretty cruel of my great-aunts to force you into something like this when you're still grieving."

Christian shifted on the sofa, now looking almost uncomfortable. "They're not forcing me," he replied, and his dark eyes met mine directly despite his obvious awkwardness. "I told them a while back that I thought I was ready to move on, but there wasn't really anyone who would have been a good match for me. They do their best to arrange marriages where the two people involved are only a few years apart at most, and it's not like there are a lot of unattached witches in their thirties in the Petrucci family."

Was I supposed to be impressed that they were so considerate in making their matches? No way.

And while I wanted to ask what the meddling Petrucci sisters would do if someone in their family was gay or asexual or nonbinary, I had a feeling an inquiry along those lines wouldn't go over very well. No doubt this unwanted witch family of mine liked to pretend those sorts of people didn't exist.

"So, because I'm thirty...." I began, and stopped. Hitting my third decade hadn't been a big deal, because I'd been with Max and had known he didn't care how old I was. Still, it continued to feel kind of strange to admit my age, as though some part of me hated to face the fact that I'd left my twenties behind.

"They thought it would be a good match," Christian finished for me. "Six years is still a bigger gap than they usually like to have, but that kind of situation begins to look a little different when you're no longer in your early twenties."

Maybe that was true. When I was that age, I'd dated here and there but hadn't been serious about anyone. How could I be, when I'd known deep in my heart that Max Sullivan was the only person for me?

"And they showed me a picture of you," Christian went on. "You're a very beautiful woman, Skye."

Color flamed in my cheeks, and I found myself wishing I'd inherited my mother's olive complexion, and not the paler skin from the O'Malley side of my family. Yes, Max called me beautiful all the time and I loved hearing him say it, but to get that kind of compliment from someone I barely knew?

It just felt weird.

"A woman who's engaged to someone else," I countered, figuring I'd better leave the "beautiful" part out of my comment.

Christian released a sigh, then reached for his glass of water. "You know the elders don't care about that."

Yes, they'd made their position patently obvious. "I'm not talking about the elders," I replied, doing my best to keep my tone as measured as his. "I'm talking about you."

A long, uncomfortable pause. Christian's fingers tapped against the side of his glass; I noticed he wasn't wearing any rings, although I thought I detected a faint band of paler skin on the fourth finger of his left hand, as though he'd worn his wedding ring for quite a while after his wife's death and had only recently decided to put it aside.

Another sign he was ready to move on, as he'd told me a few minutes earlier. A terrible paranoid side of my brain had been whispering that maybe there wasn't a dead wife, that he'd made up the whole story in order to appear sympathetic to me, but I doubted he would have gone to the trouble to have his hand look as if it had once worn a wedding ring.

"I don't like it," he said, "but this is how the Petrucci family operates. The elders make their decisions, and the rest of us have to abide by them. The last thing I wanted was to break up someone's engagement, but from the outside, it sure looks as though your life hasn't been very fun these past few months."

That comment made me bristle, even as I was forced to admit to myself that he had a point. Obviously, I loved every moment I spent with Max, but at the same time, dodging the paparazzi was getting really old. He'd assured me they'd let up once the wedding was a done deal...but what if they didn't?

Then you'll handle it, I told myself. *Being with Max is worth a few minor inconveniences.*

True. At the same time, though, I couldn't exactly tell Christian that he was way off base here.

"I'll admit I'm biased," he continued. "Some paparazzi were chasing Leonardo DiCaprio, who has an apartment in New York, when they plowed into the intersection where my wife was crossing the street. She never had a chance."

"Oh, my God," I said, knowing I sounded genuinely shocked. "That's horrible."

"It was," Christian responded. His jaw was tense, and I could tell he was doing his best to keep a tight rein on his emotions. "Luckily, the bastard was convicted on vehicular manslaughter charges, and since he already had several marks on his record because of a couple of near-misses, the judge gave him the maximum sentence. It'll be at least another ten years before he gets out."

Well, I supposed that was something, although a lengthy prison sentence still couldn't bring back Christian's wife.

"So maybe that's another reason why I agreed to go along with my aunts' plans," he added. "I guess I feel like maybe I'm swooping in to rescue you from a lifetime of being chased by those people. Because they never let up."

No, they didn't. Sure, if they decided you were boring—as they did after Max settled down in Las Vegas and began living a quiet life, before the two of us were engaged—then they might leave you alone for a while. Now, though...now that our engagement was public and our wedding imminent, even the smallest out-of-focus snapshot was probably worth a couple of hundred bucks to the photographers who'd been trailing us these past five months.

"No, they don't," I agreed, then went on, "but

I knew that going into this. I love Max, and if a few photographers weren't going to chase me away from him, then a couple of witches sure as hell aren't, either."

Christian only shook his head. "You wouldn't say that if you knew what they were capable of."

A little shiver of worry went down my spine, but I did my best to ignore it. "Well, then, enlighten me. What do I have to worry about from the big, bad witches?"

He didn't smile. "They're playing nice right now—"

"You call this nice?" I interjected. "Taking me away from Max, sending some random guy to my house to try to change my mind about marrying him?"

Expression still grim, Christian replied, "Yes, it is nice...for them. They're trying to give you space to come around to their way of thinking. But if they'd wanted to, they could have zapped you right back to New York and kept you trapped there until you changed your mind."

"Nothing will ever change my mind," I said stoutly, and now he at last gave me a tight little smile.

"Torture might."

I stared at Christian, wanting to think I hadn't heard him properly. "*Torture?*" I repeated.

He set down his glass. "Oh, I'm not talking

about waterboarding or anything that crude. I'm talking about an itch in the center of your back that won't go away no matter what you do, or the sound of a fly buzzing in your ear all day and all night. Small things—but the kind of small torment designed to have you agree to anything if only it would stop."

Yes, those irritations sounded insignificant on the surface, but considering the way my entire body flinched whenever a fly buzzed too close to my ear, I knew it would be utter torture in the truest form of the word to hear one twenty-four hours a day. My back wanted to spasm just thinking about it.

"And you'd be okay with having a wife who was tortured into marrying you?" I demanded.

"Of course not!" he burst out, then settled against the back of the couch again, as if embarrassed that he'd lost control for a moment. "I told the elders as much. But they think if they can just get you away from Max for a while, you'll see reason and decide you'd be much better off with me."

Clearly, neither Isabella nor Carmela nor Vittoria had ever truly been in love, or they wouldn't have deluded themselves into believing such a thing.

"That's never going to happen," I said flatly.

A long pause, during which Christian stared across the coffee table at me.

"No," he said at last. "I don't think it will. I'll just let myself out." A pause, and then he added quietly, "I'm sorry about all this."

He got up from the sofa and went to the door before I could say anything.

Then again, what was there to say? You couldn't turn love off and on like water from a spigot. I loved Max, and even the threat of torture wasn't enough to keep me from loving him until the day I died.

No slam, just sound of the door closing quietly. A few seconds later, I heard the distinctive creak of the third step, the one I'd never wanted to have fixed because it reminded me too much of all the things I loved about this house.

The windows were shut, so I couldn't hear Christian's car leave. All the same, I waited on the couch for a few minutes to make sure he was truly gone before I pulled the curtain aside and peered out the window, just to be safe.

But the street in front of my house was empty, so I let out a quiet little breath. Not exactly one of relief, because I knew this wasn't over.

No, I feared it had only just begun.

Protective Services

Christian Petrucci had been gone only a few minutes before panic set in. Not over my own health and safety—I figured I could deal with a little torture if necessary—but about what might be happening to Max.

What if my evil great-aunts found out I'd turned Christian down and decided the only way this marriage was going to happen was if they got rid of my fiancé?

I grabbed my iPhone and sent a quick text.

Everything quiet over there?

Max must have been camped on his phone, hoping to hear from me now that I was home from work, because his answer came back at once.

Very. How're you holding up?

I'm okay.

Then I paused, wondering whether I should

mention Christian's visit. But no—I'd told myself I needed to be honest with Max at all times, even if the truth I was telling turned out to be painful.

Christian was just here. He seems to be a decent guy, but I told him this wasn't happening. But now I'm worried about what my great-aunts might do to you.

Not even a single second of hesitation.

I'm fine. And there's no sign of anyone snooping around the ranch. Lou and Al are both on high alert, and I asked Gordon to put in some O.T. by spelling them this weekend so there are two people keeping watch all the time.

Under normal circumstances, I would have thought those precautions were more than adequate. All three men were extremely capable— and also seemed as if any one of them would be more than willing to put you through a wall if you looked at them the wrong way.

Problem was, we weren't dealing with some over-zealous paparazzi here. Instead, our adversaries were a trio of unscrupulous witches who weren't the type to take no for an answer. Even working together, there was no way Lou and Al and Gordon would be able to stop them.

However, I wouldn't bother to point out that uncomfortable truth to Max. There wasn't anything more he could really do, and if he felt better to have three bodyguards rather than the usual two, then at least he'd have some peace of mind, wouldn't be stressing out the entire time.

I also tried to reassure myself that the Petrucci witches wouldn't attempt to strong-arm me this early in the game. Of course, they wanted me to end up with Christian, but we still had a week until the wedding. They probably wanted to play nice and hope they'd wear me down in the end.

Which would never happen, obviously, but....

Although I didn't really want to admit such a thing to myself, I knew deep down that if my great-aunts had learned of my existence a year or so earlier, had presented Christian to me before Max had returned to Las Vegas and I'd learned that he loved me as much as I loved him, then Christian Petrucci might not have seemed like such a bad alternative. He was handsome and appeared kind, and back then, I very well might have told myself I could do a lot worse, especially since my dating life had been an utter wasteland at the time.

But I needed to reply to Max's text.

I'm glad it's quiet over there. I really don't know what my great-aunts are planning, but it can't be anything good. Just...keep your guard up.

You, too. Wish I could be there with you.

Wish I could be with you.

God, how I wished it. But that wasn't happening...at least, not until I could come up with some way to outsmart my evil great-aunts.

Despite all the turmoil, I realized I was hungry and needed to go out to get something to eat, since I'd come home to a house with no food. I'd cleaned out the cupboards and the fridge and taken everything with me when I moved to Max's ranch, and there simply wasn't anything here.

And even though it might have been smarter to drive over to Walmart and stock up on some staples, I didn't think I could face the Friday evening crowds at my town's biggest store. No, I'd head over to The Skillet and get myself some tacos to tide me over, and then the next morning, I'd go shopping after I woke up. Levitation Latte was closed on the weekend, so at least I'd have some time to myself to figure out what the hell I was going to do about this mess.

Because it was a Friday night, the restaurant was packed, and I had to park around the block. Doing so sent a little chill down my spine, since the last time I'd done something like this, I was attacked by a murderer trying to cover his tracks.

But Justin Hale would be in prison for a long time, and with Isabella's spell running interference, I knew I wouldn't need to worry about any paparazzi trying to assault me as I emerged from the restaurant with a bag of tacos in hand.

Or at least, I didn't think I would. However, as I walked out the door, tacos in one hand and a go-cup of iced tea in the other, I was blinded by a flash going off in my face.

"Any comments on your upcoming wedding?" a man's voice asked, and I blinked.

Standing a few feet away was Nathan O'Rourke, the one paparazzo who'd been a particular thorn in Max's and my side.

I blinked again. What the hell? How had he gotten past Isabella's spell?

"Do you really think it's a good idea to be eating tacos a week before your wedding?" he asked, and popped another shot of my most likely bemused face.

"No comment," I managed, wishing I had the guts to tell him what I thought about a guy trying to shame a woman for eating a real meal when apparently she should be on a starvation diet to fit into a size-zero wedding gown.

That was all I was able to get out, though, because in the next instant, a man's fist came out of nowhere and caught Nathan O'Rourke on the side of the jaw, knocking him to the sidewalk in front of the restaurant. For just the barest second, I thought Max had somehow come to my rescue, but then I blinked and realized my savior was Christian Petrucci, not my fiancé.

"Are you okay?" Christian asked, expression both earnest and worried at the same time.

"I'm fine," I said. Where the hell had *he* come from? I knew the men in the Petrucci family weren't able to teleport, but how on earth could he have gotten here otherwise?

I didn't have a chance to ask any questions, though, because Nathan O'Rourke had just staggered to his feet, one hand lifting to feel his reddened jaw. He was probably in his late thirties or early forties, kind of attractive in a rough-edged sort of way—I had the impression he probably imagined himself some kind of intrepid photojournalist, rather than a sleaze who profited off other people's celebrity—but right then, his pale gray eyes were blazing fire.

"What the hell?" he spluttered. "I'm going to sue your ass off for that, you son of a bitch!"

"He was just protecting me," I put in. No, I wasn't too worried about Nathan suing Christian —I had a feeling the Petruccis could afford some very good lawyers—but on the other hand, it seemed a much better idea to try to de-escalate the situation if possible.

"Yeah, and why would he have an interest in doing that?" Nathan shot back. "You got a side piece or something?"

I bristled at the insinuation in those words, but Christian spoke first. "I'm her cousin, in town for the wedding. And yeah, I'm going to hassle someone who's harassing a member of my family."

This was nothing more than the truth...even if Christian had left out a few important details...and I had a feeling that Nathan, for all his character flaws, could at least recognize that my cousin wasn't making up his story.

Not that it helped.

"You'll hear from my lawyer," Nathan snapped, and stalked away toward his red Jeep Wrangler, which was parked on the other side of the street.

An empty threat? It wasn't as though Nathan even knew who Christian was...except for the part where he'd said he was my cousin. I had a feeling as dogged a paparazzo as Nathan O'Rourke probably wouldn't have too hard a time digging up Christian's identity.

A million more questions swirled in my brain, but I knew better than to get into it on the sidewalk in front of The Skillet, especially since I could tell people had clustered near the front windows, trying to get a better look at the altercation that had just gone down outside the restaurant. "Let's go," I said. "We can talk about this at the house."

And without waiting for Christian to reply, I turned on my heel and hurried away. Out of the corner of my eye, I caught a glimpse of him standing there on the sidewalk for a second or two, as if he wasn't sure whether to follow me. To my relief, though, he appeared to decide it was a better idea to let me drive myself, because he walked over to a white Camry that was also parked across the street, and got in.

Thank God. At least this way I'd have a chance to eat my now-lukewarm tacos on the drive home.

———

I DIDN'T SEE THE CAMRY WHEN I GOT BACK to my house—I had a feeling the car was a rental, because Christian felt more like an Audi or Mercedes kind of guy—and that made me feel a little better. Not that I was probably going to get a lot of breathing room, but this gave me a minute or two to try to regain my composure.

Not much more than that, though, because I'd barely gulped down a couple of swallows of my iced tea before the doorbell rang. I put the go-cup down on a coaster, breathed in again to try to steady myself, then went to open the door.

"I can explain—" Christian began, and I frowned.

"You'd better."

Annoyed as I was, I still made myself step out of the way so he could come inside the house.

Once he was there, I closed the door but remained standing near it, my arms crossed.

"So, are you stalking me?"

He looked contrite. Or at least, I thought he did. At this point in the game, I didn't know Christian Petrucci well enough to be able to accurately read his every expression.

"I wouldn't call it 'stalking,'" he replied. "But I was worried about you. I had a feeling you were probably going to go out to get something to eat, and I thought I'd better make sure you wouldn't be harassed, since you were by yourself."

That explanation still sounded kind of stalker-y to me, even if his motivations had been pure. And also....

"I didn't need protection," I said. "Isabella cast a spell to keep the paparazzi away from me."

Now Christian's eyebrows lifted. "Then her spell wasn't working."

"But it was," I returned. "I mean, it was working earlier today. It was really obvious to me when I was walking around downtown this afternoon that the paparazzi were staying a lot farther away from me than they normally would have if I didn't have any of my bodyguards with me."

This recitation made Christian look a little flummoxed. "That doesn't make sense. When Isabella casts a spell, it works until she tells it to stop working. And I can't see why she would want a spell like that to not work. Otherwise, she wouldn't have cast it in the first place."

He was right—none of this made sense.

Except...had she shut the spell off temporarily just so Christian could come to my rescue, could play my knight in shining armor? I could see how she might think something like that would make me soften a little toward him.

But unless I could get in Isabella's face and demand why she'd turned off her spell, this mystery wasn't getting cleared up any time soon. Problem was, I had no way of getting in touch with her. It wasn't as if she'd given me her cell phone number.

I did still have Alicia's number programmed into my phone, although I didn't think reaching out to her would do me much good. She'd made herself scarce since that first visit to warn me about my aunts, and I had no idea whether she was even still in town.

"Well, spell or not," Christian said, "it was pretty obvious that that photographer was getting in your face. I didn't mean to punch him, but I was just so angry...."

He stopped there, as if he didn't know quite what to say next. I thought I understood; he really didn't seem like the sort of man who would go around socking random strangers in the jaw, but after he'd lost his wife in such a terrible way, it didn't appear too strange to me that he would lose control when he saw another paparazzo harassing the woman he was hoping would become a part of his life.

Some people might have said that flare of violence was a red flag, and yet I didn't think so. Christian Petrucci didn't seem like a rage-filled person, and had only acted out because the paparazzi were a real trigger for him. On the other hand, I didn't need him to fight my battles. There was only one man in the world I'd allow to play white knight for me, and he sure wasn't Christian.

"It's okay," I said. "I guess we should be glad he didn't call the cops."

"He still might," Christian responded, although he didn't look too worried.

I supposed it was possible that Nathan would report the incident to the police. On the other hand, Mr. O'Rourke probably knew as well as any of his fellow photographers that the Las Vegas P.D. weren't particular fans of theirs, and would probably dismiss the charges as a "he said, she said" kind of situation. For all I knew, that was why Nathan had sounded as though he preferred to lawyer up rather than rely on the cops to take Christian to task for what he'd done.

"Well, I guess you'll have to deal with that if it happens," I said, adding, "but I'll be happy to make a statement to Chief DeVargas that you were just stepping in to protect me from a photographer who got out of hand."

While Christian didn't shrug, I still got the impression he wasn't too concerned about any possible repercussions that might follow his actions.

Maybe he figured Isabella or one of her sisters would turn Nathan into a frog if he got too cocky.

"Anyway," I went on, "thanks...I guess...for stepping in. But now I just want a quiet evening at home. Things were a little crazy today."

That was for sure. If someone had asked me at 5 a.m. how I thought my day was going to progress, it definitely wouldn't have included getting blocked from eloping and having the supposed husband the Petrucci elders had chosen for me punching a paparazzo in the jaw.

I supposed it was a point in Christian's favor that he didn't try to protest and instead only gave a single nod.

"Take care of yourself," he said simply, then let himself out.

———

DESPITE MY POLICY OF TELLING MAX about everything going on in my life, I really wasn't sure whether I should let him know about what had happened in front of The Skillet earlier this evening.

I should have guessed that Las Vegas's all-too-effective gossip network would have done the work for me.

My phone rang only a few minutes after Christian left.

"Now the guy is punching people on your behalf?" Max demanded.

"It wasn't like that," I said, then paused. "Okay, maybe it was sort of like that, but it wasn't like I asked Christian to sucker-punch Nathan O'Rourke. He just came out of nowhere."

"So...Christian wasn't with you?" Max asked, his tone altering subtly.

"No," I said. Although I knew my fiancé was one of the least jealous people on the planet, I also realized he'd been pushed to just about his limit today. "I went to The Skillet by myself to get some tacos, and I'm here at home alone. Christian got pissed off at Nathan because the guy had his camera practically shoved up my nose when I came out of the restaurant. I told him I could fight my own battles, and he's gone. I don't know where he's staying, so I can't really tell you any more than that."

A silence that felt as though it went on a second or two too long. Then Max said, "But you're okay."

"I'm fine," I said. "I mean, right now I feel like you must have in *Bait and Switch* when you were dragged behind that car for a mile or whatever, but

I'm doing okay. Honestly, I'm just going to watch some TV and then go to bed early."

"I wish I could be there with you."

So did I. Yes, I loved living at the ranch, but there had been something special about the time before we moved in together, and he'd come over to the house and we'd have dinner and simply hang out, trying to act as though he was a regular guy and not someone who was one of the world's top three box-office draws.

"Soon," I said, then added, "or maybe it'll be me there with you at the ranch. Anyway, we're going to get this figured out."

A lot of guys probably would have said, *I hope so*. But Max was a perennial optimist, so he only replied, "I know we will. Enjoy your quiet evening, and try to dream of me. I know I'll be dreaming of you."

"Always," I promised, and we ended the call there.

Sometimes my dreams showed me the past, sometimes the future. I could only hope that tonight they would show me a way out of this mess.

AS FAR AS I COULD RECALL, I DIDN'T SEEM to have dreamed of anything in particular. All the same, I awoke refreshed and feeling much better than I probably should have, considering everything I had hanging over my head.

But I pushed all that to the back of my mind, telling myself I'd worry about it after I had some caffeine in my system. I didn't have all my coffee-making equipment here at the house, but while my cupboards were mostly bare, I'd left behind a little baggie of various teas, and I figured some English Breakfast should be enough to perk me up a bit. After that, I'd decide on the best time to head over to Walmart and get a few essentials. Maybe to some people, doing so would look like I'd given up, but I still had to eat while I was stuck here at the house, trying to figure out what to do about the Petrucci witches.

However, I'd only been sitting at the kitchen table for about ten minutes, my cup of tea partway drained, when my cell phone rang. I'd left it on the countertop, so I had to set down my cup and hurry over to grab the phone before the call went to voicemail.

I didn't even look at the screen, worried haste making me pick up the phone and hold it right to my ear. After all, no one called at eight-fifteen on a Saturday morning unless they were reaching out about something terribly urgent.

"Max," I said, "are you okay?"

"This isn't Max," came Isabella Petrucci's irritated tones. "This is your great-aunt. I need you to come see me right away."

"Why?" I said, mystified. "I haven't even showered yet. If this is about me turning down Christian—"

"It's about Christian, but not in the way you think," she broke in. "That photographer—Nathan O'Rourke—was found dead last night.

"This morning, your police chief arrested Christian for O'Rourke's murder."

CHAPTER 7

Leverage

The first thought that popped into my head after hearing about Christian's arrest was to wonder what the hell Isabella Petrucci expected me to do about it. However, I didn't have a chance to reply, because she went on, "We already have him out on bail, so that's something. However, we absolutely have to find some way to prove that Christian had nothing to do with Nathan O'Rourke's death."

"Why was he arrested in the first place?" I asked, although I already had a feeling I knew the answer.

"There were quite a few witnesses to that little altercation Christian had with Mr. O'Rourke in front of the restaurant yesterday," Isabella replied, something in her tone seeming to indicate she thought Christian dashing to my rescue was all my fault.

But I wasn't about to assume guilt for something Christian had done of his own free will. "And Chief DeVargas thought that was enough of a motive to make Christian kill the guy?"

"That appears to be her line of reasoning, yes," Isabella said. "Obviously, it's all utter nonsense, but we need to decide what to do next. Be at the Plaza Hotel in ten minutes so we can come up with a strategy to deal with this mess."

The call ended there, and I stared down at my phone in consternation. Ten minutes? She seriously expected me to be dressed and to drive halfway across town in such a short amount of time when I'd barely just rolled out of bed?

Yes, apparently she did.

Fuming, I took my phone with me upstairs, where I quickly brushed my teeth and washed my face, pulled my hair back into a ponytail, and dabbed on a bit of mascara and some lip gloss so I wouldn't look completely like road kill. Jeans, one of my black tops and a pair of black flats, purse grabbed as I sailed out the door. It had all taken me more like seven or eight minutes, but still, I figured I'd only be about five minutes late getting to the hotel.

Because it was still so early and none of the shops on Bridge Street were open yet, I was able to find a parking place easily enough. As I strode down the sidewalk toward the hotel, though, I couldn't quite hold back a wave of uneasiness.

Exactly what did Isabella Petrucci expect me to do about all this?

I had no idea, but I assumed I'd find out soon enough.

She'd left instructions with the woman working at the front desk to send me right up, so I mounted the steps to the second floor, barely breaking my stride. One question answered—at least now I knew where Isabella and her sisters had been hanging out while they were in town. I honestly hadn't known for sure whether they were staying here at all, or whether they'd been content with remaining in New York and teleporting back and forth as necessary.

But apparently they wanted to be close to the action, hence the hotel room.

Or hotel rooms, I discovered when Isabella answered my knock, since the doors that connected the adjoining rooms stood open, making one big space. Carmela and Vittoria lurked in the background—as did Christian, and, to my surprise, my mother. I wasn't sure what to make of her presence here, and I found my eyes narrowing.

Isabella shut the door behind me and ushered me into the room, saying, "I thought it best if we all got together and brainstormed some solutions.

Our attorney has been apprised of the situation—
he's another Petrucci cousin—but still, I think
we're all hoping we can get this settled long before
the case goes to court."

I looked past her to the place where Christian
stood a few feet away. He didn't look too worse for
wear, telling me he probably hadn't spent much
time at the police station, just enough to get
booked and to post bail.

"Are you okay?" I asked, and he gave me a
small nod.

"I'm fine," he said. "Just irritated that this is
even happening."

No kidding. I'd be equally upset if I were in his
position. Right now, though, we needed to get to
the bottom of Nathan O'Rourke's death, because I
didn't think Christian had any more to do with it
than I did.

"What happened to Nathan O'Rourke?" I
asked then.

I'd addressed the question to the room at large,
but it was Isabella who answered. "He was bludgeoned to death. Someone found his body in his
Jeep, which was parked at the Best Western hotel
where he's been staying."

Although I certainly didn't like the man, I
couldn't quite keep myself from cringing at hearing
the details of his death. "Do the police think he was

killed there, or was he murdered somewhere else and his body left in the car?"

"Chief DeVargas didn't provide those details," Christian replied. "She just kept asking me about my beef with Nathan O'Rourke, and where I was last night."

"Which was…?"

"He was here at the hotel with us," Carmella broke in, although I'd addressed the question to Christian. "We all had dinner and went to our respective rooms."

This time, I made sure to be looking straight at Christian when I spoke, just in case any of my great-aunts thought it was her turn to answer for him. "Is your room here on the second floor, too?"

"No," he said at once. "It's up on the third floor. There wasn't one available on this level."

"And what did you do after dinner?"

He shoved his hands in his pants pockets. Like yesterday, he was wearing tailored slacks and a button-up shirt, although the blazer seemed to have been abandoned for the moment. "Nothing. I went upstairs and watched some TV, then went to bed."

Exactly what I'd been worried about. "So, there isn't anyone who can corroborate your where-abouts?" I asked then, knowing I probably sounded way too much like a private eye. "Did you use your phone to make any calls or texts?"

"No," Christian replied, expression growing dejected. "There wasn't anyone I needed to reach out to, and after everything that had happened yesterday, I just wanted to have a quiet evening."

Great. Just great. My gut was telling me that Christian Petrucci couldn't have killed Nathan O'Rourke, but I could see why Chief DeVargas might view the situation very differently. His alibi was about as shaky as they came.

To my surprise, my mother stepped forward then, looking almost triumphant. "You see?" she said. "I told you Skye would be the perfect person to help out. She has an amazing talent for solving murders."

How she knew that, I wasn't sure, since the last time we'd seen each other, I'd only cracked two local murder cases. Now I had more experience under my belt, but....

I figured I'd leave that conundrum aside for later. "That's why you called me here?" I asked. "You want me to figure out who really killed Nathan O'Rourke?"

"That was the idea," Isabella said crisply. "If we can present your police chief with the real culprit, then she and the district attorney will have to drop the charges. Since it appears as if you have some talent in this area, you seem like the natural person to ask."

Of course I'll help, bubbled to my lips, but a

cannier, wilier part of my brain managed to hold back the words.

Instead, I said, "I'll see what I can do...but I have some conditions."

"'Conditions'?" Vittoria put in, looking incredulous. "You have conditions for helping a member of your own family?"

"I do," I said coolly. "Sorry if I'm not exactly overbrimming with familial loyalty right now, but you all have put me in kind of a tough spot."

Was that a ghost of a smile touching Christian's lips? I didn't want to be too obvious about staring, but it sure looked to me as though he'd already guessed where I was going with this.

"Some might say Christian is the one in the tough spot," Carmela remarked, her tone acid, although her older sister only stood there in silence, as though she also had an inkling as to what I planned to do with the unexpected leverage I'd been given.

"He is," I agreed. "Anyone want to tell me why he was in that spot in the first place? I thought the spell you cast was supposed to keep the paparazzi away from me."

Now Carmela flicked a glance at Isabella, as though waiting for her to respond. However, the older woman's lips only tightened, and I guessed she wasn't about to tell me what I'd already suspected, that Isabella had let the spell lapse precisely because she'd wanted Nathan O'Rourke to get all up in my business so Christian could come to my rescue.

What a witch.

"Anyway," I went on, after it became blatantly obvious that Isabella wasn't going to confess all, "I didn't say I wouldn't help Christian. I'm just saying that I have a few...conditions."

She planted her hands on her hips. Like her sisters, she wore all black, in her case, a straight skirt and a blouse with so much intricate embroidery and pleating, it looked almost like an antique. She definitely wasn't trying to hide her witchiness, that was for sure.

"What do you want, Skye?" she said.

Was that a hint of grudging respect in her tone?

No, I was probably imagining things.

"I want you to back off this whole Christian thing," I replied, then sent him a quick glance, one which I hoped conveyed the idea that none of my maneuvering was personal. "Christian, you seem like a really nice guy, but this just isn't going to happen."

He nodded. "I completely understand."

"We are not going to agree to any such thing —" Vittoria spluttered, but Isabella held up a hand.

"What else, Skye?"

"You'll let me go back to Max's ranch," I went

on. Yes, I'd have to backtrack on what I'd told Deanne about the situation, but I could simply tell her I'd realized I didn't want to be apart from my fiancé during these last few crucial days. After all, didn't brides often get a little dithery the closer they got to their weddings?

Anyway, I'd just have to hope she bought my story.

Isabella didn't say anything, and had an air of waiting to hear the worst, so I figured I might as well keep going.

"In fact, you're going to let my life go back to exactly what it was," I said. "In exchange, I'll do whatever I can to get Christian off the hook."

A long silence fell after I made my final demand. Both Carmela and Vittoria were silent, anxiously watching their sister, as if they knew this was her decision to make. All three of them might have been elders, but it seemed pretty clear to me that Isabella was first among equals when it came to her position in the Petrucci family.

"Very well," she said at length. "But these conditions only hold if you are able to get Christian exonerated before your wedding. If not, our deal is null and void, and you will marry him after all. A quick marriage, one that will be consummated before he stands trial. Understood?"

No pressure, I thought. Part of me quailed at the task that lay ahead—I knew absolutely nothing about Nathan O'Rourke, and therefore didn't have the slightest idea who would have had a motive for murdering him—but I also knew I didn't have much of a choice. Either I turned my sleuthing skills up to eleven, or I was marrying Christian Petrucci. It seemed pretty obvious that Isabella was less worried about a family member going to jail for a murder he didn't commit, and far more concerned with making sure he knocked me up before he was sent away for life.

The whole thing was absolutely cringe-inducing, but I knew she wouldn't budge. Not when it meant possibly adding another witch to the Petrucci family.

Which meant I absolutely had to find the person who'd killed Nathan O'Rourke...and fast.

"Understood," I said, doing my best to ignore the sinking sensation in the pit of my stomach.

If this went wrong...it would go very, *very* wrong.

"SHE LET YOU OFF THE HOOK?" MAX ASKED, expression incredulous.

"Under certain conditions," I replied. "If I don't find Nathan's killer...."

"You will," Max said, his tone one of utter conviction. "You always do."

We were sitting on the patio at his ranch, with golden hills all around and blue sky above. April in northern New Mexico wasn't always kind enough to allow us to be outside like this, but the mild weather had continued with no end in sight.

After Isabella and I made our agreement, I left the hotel and drove to the house, then closed everything up and headed over to the ranch. I'd thought about calling, but then figured it was probably better if I told Max about all these latest developments in person. Since Alicia had basically evaporated following the convo, I hadn't gotten the chance to talk to her privately.

"And if I don't figure out who killed Nathan, I'll still have to marry Christian," I said gloomily. "The horrible thing is that I get the feeling Isabella doesn't even care if he goes to prison as long as she gets a Petrucci grandbaby out of it."

Max reached over and touched my hand. "That's not going to happen," he said, his tone firm. "And she must care at least a little, or she wouldn't have agreed to let you find his killer in exchange for letting you off the hook about marrying him."

Maybe so. I honestly couldn't see exactly what her endgame was, except that I supposed forcing me to marry Christian before he was sent to the lock-up was her way of throwing a Hail Mary pass. Better for him to be a free man...and not have the

Petrucci name dragged through the mud...but if not, then at least she would have ensured that I'd contributed to the continuation of the family's bloodline.

Exactly what she'd do in those circumstances if I had a boy, and not a girl who carried the magical Petrucci gene, I didn't know.

Well, I'd just have to make sure I never had a chance to find out.

"You're probably right," I said. "Anyway, at least we'll get to be together, so I won't have to try explaining why I suddenly decided to start sleeping at my old house again."

"And I'll help you every way I can," Max assured me. "But I really think you need to close the shop this week. There's no way you can be at work eight hours a day, handle the wedding prep, *and* find Nathan O'Rourke's killer, all at the same time."

As much as I didn't like the idea, I had to agree. But making sure I ended up married to Max was the most important thing, and since I'd already floated the idea that the coffee shop might not be open the week before our wedding, most people wouldn't think there was anything strange about me deciding it was going to be too much after all.

"Okay," I said, since I knew there wouldn't be any point in arguing. "I'll put together some signs and stick them up in the shop window sometime this weekend. And I'll let Deanne know—she and her mom can help get the word out."

There hadn't been any question of asking Deanne to hold down the fort on her own, since she had way too much work to do regarding the wedding as well. Also, although her customer service skills were probably better than mine and she made very good coffee, she'd never been able to turn out muffins and pastries that were anywhere close to what I baked. No, it was better just to close down for now.

Max's bright blue eyes had an approving gleam in them. "That sounds good. Then we can get down to the work of figuring out who would have had a motive to kill Nathan O'Rourke."

"That's probably a lot of people," I said gloomily. "I have to believe a guy like that probably pissed off a whole bunch of his victims along the way."

"I'm sure he did," Max replied, looking completely undeterred. "But the nice thing about annoyed people is that they're usually open to talking about the person who did them wrong. I'll have Lou start compiling a list of anyone who's filed a lawsuit against O'Rourke because of his shenanigans. Most of the time, those things don't go anywhere, because the paparazzi always bring up their First Amendment rights even when it's clear they're infringing on people's privacy, but there should still be a record of any legal action against him."

Oh, I loved that man of mine. I hadn't even thought about attacking the problem from that angle, but he was right. Maybe it wouldn't lead to anything, but on the other hand, we might stumble across a couple of helpful clues.

"That sounds perfect," I said, and reached for my coffee. Lou had brewed a new pot upon my arrival, and also served up some awesome biscuits. Maybe they weren't *quite* as good as mine, but accompanied by some butter and some of my own blackberry preserves, they tasted like heaven.

Or maybe heaven was simply being here with Max, and knowing he was going to do whatever he could to ensure we stayed together and could enjoy mornings like this for the rest of our lives.

First, though, we had to catch a murderer.

CHAPTER 8

Heading West

"You're back at the ranch?" Deanne asked, her tone incredulous. "But you said—"

"I know what I said," I cut in. This whole situation probably made me sound like a first-class idiot, but I wasn't about to carry on with that ridiculous fiction about wanting to feel old-fashioned on my wedding day. "It's just that I realized pretty quickly what a stupid idea it was for me to be at the house and away from Max. I guess I was kind of overwhelmed by everything and wasn't thinking straight."

"Well, I can't blame you for that," she said. "I mean, the wedding would be enough to handle on its own, but now this cousin of yours is being accused of that photographer's murder? It's crazy."

"Yes, it is," I responded, even as I thought we'd gone way beyond crazy in this insane scenario.

"And I told my great-aunts I'd do whatever I could to find out what really happened to Nathan O'Rourke."

Usually, Deanne was all too happy to have me take on a new murder investigation, because doing so added a little spice to our otherwise ordinary lives. Now, though, her tone was dubious as she said, "Are you sure you're going to have time for that? I mean, with dealing with the shop and your wedding only a week away?"

"I decided to close the shop early after all," I told her. "Because you're right—it's way too much. But I'll pay you anyway, obviously."

She made a dismissive sound, although I had a feeling she was inwardly relieved. Mike's salary would have been enough to support them without her income from Levitation Latte...barely...but the combination of her regular pay and half the tips we got at the shop allowed them to have a nice house and newish cars, and to go on vacation once a year. Having to give up a week's salary without any warning would have definitely forced them to tighten their belts a little.

I had no intention of impacting their lifestyle, though. Yes, it would be kind of a stretch for me to pay her when there wasn't any money coming in, although I had enough of a cushion put aside that things would be okay.

And then I wanted to laugh at myself for even

entertaining such a notion. If I came up short, Max would step in and probably give me double what I needed to cover the lost revenue from the extra week I'd be closed. He'd always been a generous person, and now that he had the kind of money that would be hard to spend in a single lifetime, he spread it around without a second thought.

"So, Max is having Lou look into a couple of things," I went on, "and we're both hoping that might give us the kind of leads we're looking for. In the meantime, though, we've got that final dress fitting in Santa Fe on Monday afternoon, and all the other bits and pieces the rest of the week."

Including my girls' afternoon out on Thursday, something I hadn't been super thrilled about but which Deanne insisted needed to be part of the pre-wedding festivities.

"I'm glad you're closing," she said, her tone firm. "Even before this whole murder thing, it just didn't make sense to me for you to try to stay open."

"Well, I'm not," I replied, then paused there, because Lou had just entered the family room where I was making the call, Max right at his heels. Since both of them wore expectant expressions, I had to believe they must have already dug up something interesting about Nathan O'Rourke. "Anyway, gotta go. If I don't talk to you before then, I'll pick you up Monday afternoon for our fitting."

"See you then," she said, and we both ended the call.

I set my phone down on the coffee table. Before I had a chance to speak, Max said, "Lou thinks he's found a couple of things."

That was pretty much what I'd been hoping for, but still, I hadn't expected any real developments this early in our investigation, and hope stirred within me. "Like what?"

The two of them came further into the room, and Max took a seat next to me on the couch, while Lou settled himself in the armchair to one side.

"Lots of people weren't too thrilled with the guy," Lou said. "But I'm looking at two real possibilities right now. One of them is Jana Donalds."

"The actress?" I replied, startled. She wasn't quite the box office star that Max was, but still, no one could claim she wasn't a household name, either. For the past couple of years, she'd starred in a string of fun rom-coms, clearly doing her best to revive the genre.

"The same," Max said. "Looks like he was getting a little too up in her personal business, so she slapped him with a restraining order. Then he countersued, telling her she was infringing on his First Amendment rights. They've been going back and forth in court for the past couple of years. She never said anything about it to me, though."

"'Never said....'" I repeated, then remembered

that Max had starred in a movie with her a couple of years ago.

Maybe someday I'd get used to the way he rubbed elbows with some of the world's richest and most famous people, but I doubted I was going to be there any time soon.

"But I could tell she was stressed about something during the shoot," Max went on, smiling a little at my befuddlement. "I didn't know her well enough to pry, so I left it alone. Still, I'm not sure we can discount her as a suspect. She might have finally hit the breaking point and decided she needed to remove the guy from her life once and for all."

"You really think Jana Donalds has the strength to beat someone over the head like that?" I asked, knowing how dubious I sounded. "Or really, any woman who isn't an Olympic bodybuilder or something?"

"Maybe not Jana herself," Lou put in. "But she could've hired someone to take care of her problem, you know? It's not outside the bounds of possibility. Lots of stuff gets swept under the rug that the general public never hears about."

I'd have to take his word for it; he'd worked in security for many years, while I was still a mostly naïve chick who'd grown up in a small town that was definitely off most people's radar. And since Max hadn't said anything to contradict his bodyguard, I had to believe he'd also heard of a few scandals that had been kept from public consumption.

Glancing over at him, I said, "Do you really think Jana Donalds is capable of that?"

He gave an uneasy lift of his shoulders. "I don't know for sure. She's not the bubbly person you see on the screen, though—she's pretty intense. I hate to think of anyone being capable of murder, but since we've run across plenty of people like that over the past year or so, let's just say I'll suspend judgment until we have all the facts in hand."

Wow. My head wanted to spin, but I told it I had more important things to focus on.

"And the other possibility?" I inquired. Even if Jana Donalds was on the list of suspects, I still wanted to think someone else must be to blame here.

"Yeah," Lou said. "Guy named Todd Anderson. He's O'Rourke's next-door neighbor in Pasadena. The two of them have been litigating for years, looks like—Anderson gets pissed off that O'Rourke is gone a lot and lets his yard go to hell, and O'Rourke has sued Anderson multiple times over a wall he says was rebuilt six inches onto his property. That lawsuit's been bounced around for years."

"Charming," I remarked, and Max grinned.

"Just another reason why I'm glad I moved out to the ranch," he said. "No neighbors to worry about. One of the houses next to mine in L.A. is owned by a music producer, and he throws some epic parties. They sound like they're pretty amazing, but it's still not the kind of thing I want to hear when I've got a 5 a.m. call."

No, probably not. I really didn't know much about Max's house in Bel-Air, except it was worth millions and he was currently having his assistant stay there rent-free to keep an eye on things. So far, he hadn't been making noises about selling it, but it was entirely possible he was waiting for interest rates to drop a little so he could attract more buyers willing to pay what it was truly worth. As far as I could tell, he'd paid cash for the place, just as he had for Sunset Ridge, so it wasn't as if he had to worry about carrying multiple seven-figure mortgages.

Still, it surprised me a little that a place in that price range was so close to the neighbors that you still had to worry about the noise they generated.

"Anyway," Lou commented, "I don't see it as outside the bounds of possibility that this Todd Anderson guy might have gotten fed up with the whole thing and come to New Mexico to get rid of his problem once and for all. I'll keep digging into that one, but Jana Donalds is someone you and Max are better off investigating yourselves."

"'Max and I'?" I repeated, not expecting that angle on things. "What, you want the two of us to go grill some movie star about a murder she might or might not have committed?"

I suppose I should have expected the broad grin that spread across my fiancé's lips. After all, he was the kind of person who didn't think twice about leaping into a situation head-first.

"I'm probably one of the few people she'd actually talk to," he said. "It's no big deal. We'll just fly out to L.A.—"

"'Just'?" I said.

His smile held steady. "Sure. The plane's already gassed up and ready to go. We'll have to land in Flagstaff to refuel, but that won't take long. And from there we can go straight to Santa Monica Airport. I'll call Courtney and have her arrange for a car to meet us there—and to reach out to Jana and see if she'll meet with us."

"If she's even around," I pointed out. "I mean, isn't it possible she's out of town on a movie shoot or a press junket or something?"

For the first time, Max appeared a little unsure of himself. But then he perked up again as he pulled his phone out of his pocket. "I'll ask Courtney to check. You're right—there wouldn't be much point in flying all the way out there if Jana is out of town."

A tense little silence fell as he sent the text. If it turned out that Jana Donalds really was off filming a movie somewhere, what would we do next?

Well, knowing Max, he'd probably just charter a jet to fly us to wherever she was currently working, whether that was in Switzerland...or the wilds of Borneo.

But then his phone pinged, and he sent Lou and me a relieved smile. "No, Jana's in town. Courtney got in touch with her assistant, and though she's going to head to New York for a press junket on Tuesday, she's in L.A. right now. Which means we need to get going."

"How long will the trip take?" I asked. After all, while I'd been in Max's Skylane a few times, puttering up to Taos or even over to Austin, Texas, wasn't anywhere close to the same thing as flying all the way to the West Coast.

"Six hours, give or take," he replied. "We'll lose a little time in Flagstaff when we refuel, but it won't hurt to get out and stretch our legs, get something to eat."

That sounded like fun to me. I'd never been to Flagstaff, although I knew by necessity that our stay there wouldn't be very long.

"And Al and Gordon and I will hold down the fort here," Lou said as Max and I got up from the couch. "If I find out anything more about the beef between Todd Anderson and Nathan O'Rourke, I'll let you know."

With all that settled, Max and I hurried off to the master bedroom to quickly pack for our impromptu trip. I had absolutely no idea what the weather in L.A. was like right now, although I assumed it must be warmer than here in Las Vegas. A quick check of the weather app on my phone told me it was currently seventy-two degrees in Santa Monica, the perfect temperature to wear just about anything.

That was why I included a pretty dark turquoise wrap dress and flats along with a pair of jeans and a couple of tops. The last thing I wanted was to show up for an audience with Jana Donalds looking like a complete schlub.

As Max drove to the local airport, I sent a quick text to Isabella, just so she'd know the two of us were being as proactive as possible.

We're following up on a lead in L.A. Should be back by Monday morning at the latest.

That wasn't just wishful thinking, either. No matter what happened in California, Deanne and I —and Darcy Montoya, a deputy with the Las Vegas P.D. and the only other woman in town I was close enough friends with to include in my wedding party—needed to be in Santa Fe at three for our final fittings at the bridal salon.

Isabella's reply came back quickly.

I'm glad to hear you're working on something. I'll pass the information along to Christian and my sisters.

No mention of my mother, but maybe Isabella

had decided it wasn't worth including her in her comment, since she wasn't the murder suspect... this time...and she wasn't a family elder, either.

But at least Christian would know Max and I were doing what we could. True, my main motivation for all this was to ensure a happy life with the man of my choosing, and yet, I certainly didn't want to see Christian in jail, either. The man had dealt with enough tragedy in his life already.

I'll stay in touch.

I hoped my brief reply was enough reassurance that Max and I really were headed to California to clear up the mystery, and not because we were trying to elope. The thought crossed my mind that maybe we should, and yet....

And yet, I'd given Isabella my word. Some people might have said she didn't deserve such consideration, but at the same time, it was one thing to try to duck out and elope when no bargains had been made between us, and something else entirely when I'd already told her I'd do whatever I could to keep Christian out of jail.

By that point, we'd reached the airport. Max parked near the hangar, then got out of the SUV so he could remove the padlock and drive the Bronco inside. The plan was to leave it here while we were gone so we could go straight from the plane to the car after we got back, thus leaving Lou and Al and Gordon to remain on duty back at the ranch.

The airport was far too small to have a tower, but there wasn't anyone else lining up to taxi down one of its two runways, which didn't surprise me too much. Out of all the other times we'd flown out of here, I'd only seen another airplane on one other occasion.

We were in the air soon enough, circling over our hometown, a greenish splotch in the otherwise golden brown landscape that surrounded the city. A couple of minutes later, we'd reached cruising altitude, the few clouds in the sky below us and the sun at our backs.

"We'll have to wait a lot longer to get a runway at Santa Monica," Max said. "Just another reason why I'm a fan of country life."

True. I had to believe there were far more people with the means to have a private airplane on L.A.'s expensive west side, rather than here in tiny Las Vegas. Mostly, the airport here was used as a refueling stop for people on their way to Denver or points even farther north or east. From what I'd been able to tell, only a rough half dozen planes, including Max's Cessna, were even kept in the hangar there.

"Well, hopefully it won't be too crowded when we leave," I replied, although I had my doubts. Even if all went well and we were able to see Jana sometime this afternoon after we landed, we wouldn't be able to head back until tomorrow...

and I had to believe the skies above L.A.'s world-famous beaches would be crowded with pilots trying to get in some flying time before they had to head back to work Monday morning.

I told myself that whatever happened, the important thing was getting Jana to open up about her problems with Nathan O'Rourke, and we'd figure out the logistics afterward. Worst-case scenario, Max and I could still fly out Monday morning and land in Santa Fe, where we could get an Uber to take me to the bridal salon so I wouldn't miss my appointment. It wouldn't be ideal, but it would be better than nothing, especially since I had no intention of making Lou or Al drive all the way down from Las Vegas just to give me a twenty-minute ride to the bridal shop.

"I guess we'll just have to see," Max replied diplomatically, which I guessed was his way of trying to let me down easy. Even though he hadn't taken up flying until he moved to New Mexico, I had to believe he'd flown out of Santa Monica on private jets plenty of times, and therefore had much more intimate knowledge of the place than I did.

We didn't talk about that, though. No, we discussed the wedding, and chatted about other places we should fly to over the summer and next fall, before bad weather effectively grounded us. He wanted to take me to Jackson Hole and Aspen and other places he'd visited but I'd never seen, and painted a picture of a future so bright and shining and beautiful, I wanted it to be true.

As with so many other things, though, I'd just have to wait and see what happened.

A little before one o'clock, we landed at Flagstaff-Pulliam Airport. It was located a ways outside the city's downtown, but since Max had me call for an Uber as we were taxiing down the runway, we didn't have to wait very long for a ride.

The city's vintage downtown was adorable, reminding me a little of Las Vegas, but with a far more mountainy feel—which made sense, considering the peaks of the snow-capped mountains that loomed above the city to the north. I didn't know their names, and since we'd only stopped here to grab lunch before heading back to the plane, I'd have to look that fact up at a later date when I didn't have so many other things fighting for attention in my brain.

From there, we followed I-40 west for a while, then altered course so we were flying in a southwesterly direction over the high deserts outside L.A.'s massive sprawl. It seemed kind of crazy to me that a place as populated as Southern California could still have so many miles of what looked like uninhabited country surrounding it.

And then I saw the deep blue gleam of the Pacific Ocean off to my right, and I couldn't help pulling in an awed breath. I'd never had much of a desire to visit the beach, had always considered myself utterly happy to live in a landscape of mountains and rolling hills, but even I had to admit the vista of wide blue ocean and bordering white beaches—thickly populated on this sunny day in April—was absolutely breathtaking.

Max must have taken note of my reaction, because his mouth quirked and he said, "It's something, isn't it?"

"It's beautiful," I breathed, then shifted in my seat so I was facing him. "How could you leave all this?"

His clear eyes were almost the same color as the sky above and the sea below. "Easy. You were there."

My heart performed a funny little skip in my chest. No matter how many times he reiterated his love for me, it always felt as though I was hearing it for the first time.

"Still...." I said, and he chuckled.

"You might not be as entranced after sitting in L.A. traffic for a while. But we're getting close—I need to focus on landing."

I nodded, and sat there quietly as he spoke to the tower and reaffirmed the coordinates he'd already set up with them a few minutes earlier as we were entering the Westside's crowded airspace. It felt a lot more tense than flying out of sleepy Las

Vegas, and I was all too glad when we were wheels down about ten minutes later, taxiing along the runway the air-traffic controller had specified.

"Courtney got us some parking space," Max told me as we turned off the runway and toward a group of hangars a few hundred yards ahead of us. "So we'll leave the plane here for the night. Oh, there she is."

He didn't point—both his hands were busy with guiding the plane toward one of the hangars in the distance—but he didn't need to. I spied a big white Range Rover parked near one of the structures, and a tall woman with sandy-blonde hair standing next to it.

Five minutes later, the plane was safely stowed in the hangar, and Max and I were carrying our bags toward the waiting woman and her white SUV. She smiled as we approached, and put out a hand.

"Hi, there," she said. "I'm Courtney Hill. So nice to finally meet you!"

"It's very nice to meet you, too," I replied. Although I'd never seen pictures of her before, Courtney was pretty much exactly what I'd expected, a quintessential California golden girl, from her streaked blonde hair to her clear blue eyes and apparently year-'round tan, tall and slender.

I wouldn't let myself be jealous, though. What for? Courtney had worked for Max for years, and it was clear their relationship was professional and nothing more.

We stowed our luggage in the storage compartment at the back of the Range Rover, and then Max and I both got in the back seat.

"Hope you don't mind playing chauffeur," he joked. "But this is Skye's first trip to L.A., and I didn't want to leave her alone in the back."

"It's fine," Courtney said, and from the bit I could see of her face in the rearview mirror, it looked like she smiled a little. "Let me get you home."

Home, I thought as she pulled away from the hangar and onto a feeder road that looked as though it emptied onto a main street. But was the Bel-Air house truly Max's home? He owned it, but he hadn't lived there for months.

However, I didn't bother to comment, only sat in the back seat, my hand in Max's, as he pointed out various sights, from stores he used to frequent to some of his favorite restaurants.

"I wish we could stay here longer," he said, "but I know this isn't exactly a vacation."

No, it wasn't. I tightened my fingers on his and replied, "Well, we'll just have to come back when we're not trying to solve a murder."

He grinned. That little exchange had been spoken in lowered voices, so I didn't think Courtney had heard any of it.

Up in the front seat, she said, "Max, I freshened up your suite, so it's ready for the two of you.
And I knew it doesn't give you much time to relax
and unwind, but Jana's assistant texted me right
before you landed and said she could see you at five
but no later than that, since she has some kind of
reception to go to."

"That's fine," Max assured his assistant. "We'll
still have enough time to stretch our legs, grab
some water or something. Can you drive us? I'm a
little out of practice with L.A. traffic."

"No problem."

He wasn't kidding about the traffic. Even
though it was a Saturday afternoon and therefore
people shouldn't have been commuting to and
from work, the streets around us were choked with
cars, and we often had to sit through two or even
three phases of a light before we could lurch ahead
to the next clogged intersection.

"This is awful," I whispered, and he only
smiled.

"Isn't it? Why do you think I just have to laugh
when people ask me whether I miss L.A.?"

I snuggled next to him, chuckling a little
myself.

But even though it felt as if we were never
going to make it to his house in Bel-Air, about
twenty minutes later we passed through an enormous set of black iron gates that Courtney acti-

vated with a push of the remote clipped to the Range Rover's sun visor, and onto a winding driveway that led up to a sprawling, quasi-modern house with two stories and lots of trees all around, lending the property a sense of privacy. However, I could see why Max had commented about hearing his neighbor's parties, because the homes here did seem closer together than I'd thought they would be, were sitting on lots of probably not much more than a half-acre each.

Courtney parked at the far end of the large, four-bay garage, and we all piled out. She made a move as if to get our luggage, and Max only shook his head at her.

"You're my assistant, not the bellman," he said. "And we're dropping in on you out of the blue."

Her eyes met mine for a second, and in that moment, I thought we made a connection. Both of us couldn't help being amused that Max would feel as if he was intruding in his own house...such an attitude was so quintessentially *him*.

"Okay, okay," she replied. "But do you want me to get you dinner reservations tonight, maybe at Spago or Maude?"

"No—but thanks," he said at once. "I think Skye and I will probably just freewheel it, see how things go with Jana first."

Judging by the way Courtney didn't bother to argue, she was obviously used to this sort of behavior from Max. Instead, she made a comment about going to her office and peeled off down a marble-floored hallway past an angular staircase, while my fiancé guided me toward those same stairs.

"We can dump everything in the bedroom and get freshened up a little," he told me as we climbed the steps.

About all I could do was nod. I'd known his house here in L.A. would be impressive, but I hadn't quite imagined this warmly modern edifice, with its expansive windows and museum-quality art hanging on the walls.

Had he really left all this behind to live on a ranch in Nowhere, New Mexico?

The main suite he guided me to didn't do much to steady my nerves, either. I estimated that the entire ground floor of my house would have fit in the space, and more of those insanely expensive bifold doors made a wall of glass on the side of the room that overlooked the backyard. A long, narrow electric fireplace had been installed on the wall opposite the bed, and the expanse in between was large enough that I probably could have parked three of my Subaru Crosstreks end-to-end to fill it.

"This is...really something," I managed as I set my weekender bag on the floor near the foot of the bed. The little nylon piece—which I'd bought at

Walmart years before—looked hopelessly out of place against the polished concrete surface.

At once, Max came over to me and took my hands in his, then kissed me on the cheek. "It's just a house."

"A house that looks like a hotel," I returned.

He chuckled and kissed me again, this time on the mouth. The usual welcome heat flushed through my body, although I knew I couldn't let myself get too distracted.

"It was an investment, nothing more," he said. "My financial planner told me I needed to buy a house, something that would appreciate. And it definitely did—I think it's worth about seven mil more now than it used to be. I really should think about selling it."

"You'd get rid of all this?" I asked, freeing one hand so I could gesture around the cavernous bedroom.

Max looked supremely unconcerned in a way only he could. "Well, I kind of already have, haven't I? I mean, I've been living on the ranch for more than a year, and I think I've spent less than a week back here in all that time. It was just a place to crash when I absolutely had to come into town to do some business."

A place to crash. That was the sort of thing you might say about a vacation condo, not a nine-bedroom monstrosity like this.

"I'll put it on the market tomorrow, if that's what you want," he added.

"That's not my call to make," I told him, and he shook his head.

"We're a team, Skye," he said. "We make our decisions together."

I looked around. Why Max hadn't brought me here before this, I wasn't sure, although I knew part of it was that he knew better than I that the paparazzi would be even more ferocious here on their home turf, whereas back in Las Vegas, we had at least a modicum of peace and quiet when we were at the ranch. At this house, even though it had gates, we couldn't hope for anywhere near the same kind of privacy.

"Then let's worry about the house later," I said. "First, we need to hear what Jana Donalds has to say."

CHAPTER 9

Little Lies

As it turned out, Jana Donalds' house wasn't too far from Max's, maybe a quarter-mile at the most. Unlike his glassy, modern mansion, though, her home was a graceful Spanish-style structure, something that looked like it might have been built during the golden age of Hollywood and then lovingly restored. It felt a little friendlier than Max's house, although that could have been personal bias speaking—I'd never had much use for modern architecture, and much preferred homes that were cozy and felt as if they had a history.

Naturally, Jana didn't answer the door herself. Like Max, she had an assistant, although the person in question here was a man maybe a few years younger than either Max or me, his bleached hair cut super short on the sides and longer on top, and wearing tailored gray slacks, a chartreuse shirt, and ostentatious horn-rimmed glasses.

"Hello, Mr. Sullivan," the man said as he opened the door. "So nice to see you again. And I assume this is your lovely fiancée?"

"Yes, this is Skye," Max replied, and reached out to give the man's hand a quick shake. "Good to see you again, Chad."

Obviously, the two had met before, which made sense. Max had worked on a film with Jana, and probably had encountered Chad on set or maybe even here at her home.

"Jana's waiting for you," Chad said, and gestured for us to follow him into the house. "It's such a nice day, she thought she should meet with you on the patio."

Yes, it was nice, even milder here than it had been in Las Vegas. The house itself was gorgeous, filled with a carefully curated mix of antiques and more modern furniture, the walls covered in landscapes that seemed to evoke the hillsides of the northern part of the state, although, since I'd never actually been to that part of California, I'd just have to go on the pictures I'd seen.

However, because Chad was walking at a decent clip through the house, which seemed nearly as big as Max's, I didn't have much time to stop and look at anything more closely. A few minutes later, we emerged onto a wide veranda that overlooked a green lawn, with large trees bordering the terrace and providing plenty of shade from the bright sun.

Jana Donalds sat at a wrought-iron table set off to one side, clearly taking advantage of the shelter from the trees. Her strawberry blonde hair was pulled back in a simple ponytail, and she wore a plain white shirt over jeans and sandals. Even though her makeup was minimal, she was still casually gorgeous in a way I knew I'd never be able to duplicate.

And I told myself that didn't matter. Obviously, I was the woman of Max's heart, or he wouldn't be here with me now.

Jana got up when we approached, and extended a hand. Her smile looked genuine enough as she said, "Hello, Skye. It's so nice to meet you."

"It's very nice to meet you, too," I replied, glad I sounded relatively normal and not like someone who was utterly starstruck at meeting a woman who'd appeared in some of my favorite movies. Up close, I got the feeling she was probably a few years older than Max or me, maybe as much as thirty-six or thirty-seven, although the age difference definitely wasn't apparent when you saw her on the screen.

The magic of Hollywood, I supposed.

"What's this about?" she asked, as she indicated that we should take a seat. Chad, who'd disappeared as the two of us stepped out onto the patio, reappeared just then, holding a silver tray and three tall glasses of iced tea.

Max and I both murmured a thank-you, although I noticed that he waited until Chad had gone back into the house before he spoke again.

"It's about that paparazzo, Nathan O'Rourke," Max said, and a flicker of surprise came and went on Jana's delicate features before she was able to control it.

However, she sounded casual enough as she said, "Oh, has he been bothering you, too? Maybe we should get a class-action lawsuit going."

"Actually, he's dead," Max said, tone flat, and now there was no mistaking the startled expression on Jana's face.

"'Dead'?" she repeated. "What happened?"

"We don't know exactly yet," I put in, figuring it was my turn to add something to the conversation. "But the police in our town—Las Vegas, New Mexico—found him dead in his Jeep. It looks like he suffered some kind of head trauma."

"That's...terrible," Jana said, and reached for her iced tea with a hand that shook a little. "But what does it have to do with me?"

"You had a restraining order against him," Max said. "Can you tell us what that was about?"

A long pause. She looked from Max to me and

back again, and then replied, "You don't think *I* had something to do with his death, do you?"

"Probably not," he said easily. "But still, we figured we should hear it from you in your own words."

Her brows pulled together, and I could tell she wasn't exactly thrilled with either of us right then. Tone a little too even, she said, "Bored with your ranch already, Max? Is that why you've decided to play amateur detective?"

"Oh, Skye's the real Sherlock Holmes here," he responded, not appearing at all put off by Jana's question. "I just tag along and play Dr. Watson. The reason why we're investigating this particular case is that a relative of hers has been implicated, and we know he's innocent. But then we got some information about the restraining order you had against O'Rourke, and it seemed like something we needed to check into."

Once again, Jana reached for her iced tea, then took a long, deliberate swallow. When she spoke, it was still in that same flat tone, as though she was doing everything she could to keep her emotions at bay. "I assume we're speaking in confidence."

"Of course," he replied at once.

Her fingers—wearing a perfect shell-pink manicure—tapped against the side of the glass. "When did this murder happen?"

"Friday night," I supplied.

She gave a small nod, as though satisfied by my reply. "Well, I have an alibi. I was at a party at Alistair Wilde's house."

The name didn't mean anything to me, but Max inclined his head slightly, as though he knew the person in question. "So, you've got plenty of people who can say you were here in L.A., and not off in New Mexico causing mayhem."

That comment elicited a small chuckle, although there was something brittle about the sound, as if Jana had known she needed to make some kind of response, and that was how it had come out.

"Exactly," she said.

"But even if you have an iron-clad alibi, the police might point out that you definitely have the means to hire someone to do your dirty work," Max went on, and his former co-star's eyes narrowed.

"You don't have a very high opinion of me, do you, Max?" she asked.

He settled against the back of his chair, tea in hand. Any casual observer would have thought he didn't have a care in the world, but I noticed how his fingers gripped the glass and knew he wasn't quite as casual as he seemed.

"This has nothing to do with an 'opinion,'" he said. "This is just about getting to the heart of the matter so an innocent man doesn't end up in prison."

Jana pressed her lips together, as if to reassure herself that the soft pink gloss she wore was still in place. "I had nothing to do with it," she said.

Her words had the ring of truth, but I'd been fooled before. "Why the restraining order?" I asked then. "What made Nathan O'Rourke different from all the other paparazzi who follow you around?"

Now she glanced away, past us to the swimming pool that took up a good chunk of the yard on the south side of the patio. Her mouth tightened again.

"He's quite aggressive," she said, and then sent Max a sly look. "But I suppose you should know that fairly well, considering how he's been tailing you all these months. I felt bad for you—but at the same time, I couldn't help being glad Nathan was a thousand miles away."

Something about the way she said the paparazzo's name felt off, as though she was talking about someone she knew well, and not a man who was only one of a horde of celebrity photographers who liked to follow her wherever she went.

Max obviously noticed the same nuance in her words, because he said, "Is there something you're not telling us, Jana?"

She didn't reply at first, only kept staring at the

pool, expression almost distracted, as if she'd just discovered a fresh batch of leaves that had drifted onto its surface, or maybe a bird swimming where it shouldn't be.

When she spoke, though, her voice was firm. "If I tell you this, it has to be in utter confidence."

"Of course," Max said, and I nodded.

"We won't say a thing to anyone."

Well, unless you're confessing a murder, I thought then. *Because I'm definitely not keeping that information from the Las Vegas P.D.*

The next words out of her mouth, however, were something I hadn't been expecting at all.

"Nathan and I had kind of a thing," she admitted, and Max and I both stared at her in shock. I couldn't see myself, of course, but I had to believe I looked just as gobsmacked as he did right then.

"You and Nathan O'Rourke?" he said, sounding utterly confounded.

"Is that so strange?" she retorted, obviously annoyed by her former co-star's reaction. "He wasn't a bad-looking man. I was bored and thought it would be fun. But then when I decided I'd gotten my wiggles out and it was time to move on, he wouldn't accept the breakup. Kept calling me, and coming to the house, and dogging me wherever I went. Most people would have thought he was just doing his job, but I knew it was a lot more than that. He was obsessed. That's why I got the restraining order."

"I'm sorry," I said.

She sent me a look that bordered on but wasn't quite contemptuous. "It's a thing that happened. Just like his death. It's too bad he went out that way, but I suppose some people would say he deserved it. Anyway, I don't know who killed him. I just know it had nothing to do with me." A pause, and then she pulled in a breath and added, "And that's all I want to say on the subject. It was nice to see you again, Max."

Well, there was a conversation-ender if I'd ever heard one. In unspoken agreement, the two of us got up from our chairs.

"It was nice to see you, Jana," he said, tone almost formal. "And don't worry—we won't say anything to anyone."

His hand found mine, and we walked back inside. Chad must have been waiting and watching, because he got up from the chair where he'd been sitting in the family room and said, "All done already?"

"Yes," I said. "Max just wanted to say hi while he was in town."

If Chad thought it a little strange that Max would spend less than fifteen minutes with his former co-star when he'd been out of town for months, he didn't show it. No, he merely ushered us to the front door, wished us a good rest of our day, and then closed the door behind us.

In silence, we walked over to the Porsche waiting in the driveway, one of the cars Max had left behind here in California. It wasn't until we'd gotten in and we were slowly pulling out of the gates that he said, "Wow."

That was one word for it. "You never had any idea she had a thing going with Nathan O'Rourke?"

"No," Max replied. "I don't think anyone did, or it would have been splashed all over the tabloids —you know, with trashy headlines like 'The Princess and the Paparazzo,' or whatever. She was probably super careful, never went anywhere with him in public, never did anything that could connect the two of them. And I believe her about ending it. We never dated, but she does like to keep her relationships short. I guess she thinks that'll make things less complicated."

Except in Nathan's case, where it had gotten so complicated, she'd had to get a restraining order against him. Anyone on the outside looking in would have thought she'd merely done so because he was getting a little too aggressive about stalking her for photographs, providing her some convenient cover.

"And you don't think she would have hired someone to kill him?" I asked then. True, she really didn't seem the type, but my past investigations had taught me never to take anything at face value.

Max shook his head, then turned the Porsche onto Glenroy Avenue, heading for his house. "I doubt it. You heard what she said. She was glad he was off in Las Vegas and staying out of her business. There would have been no reason for her to hire someone to kill him...not that I think she's even capable of doing that kind of thing. No, she was just happy to have him out of her hair."

And maybe part of the reason Nathan had been so steadfast about staying in New Mexico rather than coming and going like a lot of the other paparazzi was that he had a very good reason to be far away from the woman who'd broken his heart.

I couldn't help experiencing a twinge of pity at that thought, even though a few days earlier, I would have said there was no way in the world I'd ever feel sorry for Nathan O'Rourke. But, as I'd discovered far too often recently, people tended to hide much more of themselves than I'd ever expected.

"Okay, so I guess we can scratch Jana Donalds off our lists," I said, hoping I sounded brisk and businesslike, and not as if I'd been harboring a secret pity for Mr. O'Rourke only a few seconds earlier. "Now what?"

"Well, I guess we have to wait and see if Lou digs up anything more about Todd Anderson,

Nathan's next-door neighbor," Max replied. Something about his tone told me he was glad of the switch to a different topic as well, as if he, too, might have been thinking about the paparazzo's reasons for sticking around in Las Vegas.

And I also found myself wondering if we should have tried to stay longer with Jana, maybe allowed her to express something of the loss she felt after hearing about Nathan's death.

Then again, she'd seemed pretty anxious to get rid of us. Her grief might have been the sort she wouldn't even admit to herself, let alone anyone else. It seemed a lot more likely that she'd tell herself to get over it, that she'd dumped him months before, and so Nathan's murder shouldn't be anything more than a sad footnote in a book she'd already placed on a shelf and forgotten.

Max pressed a button on the remote clipped to the Porsche's sun visor as we approached the driveway, and we pulled past the sleek black metal gates and into the garage. In addition to the Porsche, an Audi SUV and a perfectly restored 1965 Mustang convertible made up the rest of his stable, with Courtney's white Range Rover sitting at the far end.

"Did you actually drive all of these cars?" I asked Max as we got out of the Carrera.

He looked a little sheepish, as though he didn't quite want to admit how extravagant he'd been with his cars when he was living here in L.A. "Off and on," he replied. "The Mustang was for nice days, and the Audi was for when I needed to cart stuff around. But I mostly drove the Porsche."

Well, at least he had a specific use for each of them. I thought of the black Bronco that was his single mode of transportation in New Mexico, and said, "Why haven't you brought any of your cars to Las Vegas? You have room."

Which was the truth. The ranch also had a four-bay garage, so he couldn't have all of his cars and still leave room for my Subaru—Al and Lou both parked their vehicles outside—but there was space for a couple of them.

"I've thought about it," he admitted, opening the door for me so I could enter the house via the kitchen. "But I couldn't decide which ones I should have. The Porsche might be a bit much for our town."

Maybe. Still....

"You seem to like it best, though," I replied. "And since you have the Bronco, you probably don't need a second SUV."

"True." Max paused in front of the kitchen's enormous island, a subtle little affair about ten feet long with a granite waterfall edge. His bright blue eyes glinted at me as he added, "Tell the truth, Skye —you just want me to drive you around town in a Carrera."

I chuckled. "You got me." My amusement didn't last very long, though, not as I realized we'd come all this way for basically nothing. "So...what do we do now?"

He came over and folded me into his arms, giving me a hug I desperately needed right then. I always felt utterly safe when he held me like that, and I could only pray he'd be able to go on doing it for the rest of our lives.

"Now," he said, "I'll show you a good time in L.A. Then tomorrow, we'll go home."

AND THAT WAS EXACTLY WHAT HE DID. No, he didn't take me to some fancy five-star restaurant, but a quiet little place over in Santa Monica where the food was amazing even if the decor and location weren't anything to write home about. It didn't matter, though, not when I was dining on the most mouth-watering grilled sea bass I'd ever had, a dish washed down with a fabulous Italian pinot grigio. No one seemed to realize who Max was, or, if they did, they didn't comment on his celebrity status or act all starstruck.

It was almost like being back home in Las Vegas.

Afterward, though, wasn't like our hometown at all, but a walk on the beach in the cool, dusky night, with a breeze off the ocean that made me glad I'd thrown a jean jacket into my overnight bag at the last minute as I was packing.

Max actually suggested going to the pier and doing something silly like playing the games in the arcades there or taking a ride on the huge Ferris wheel, but I'd declined. The pier was a much more public place than the dimly lit beach, and I'd worried that someone would recognize him and turn our fun little outing into a three-ring circus.

I'd actually wondered at the complete lack of any paparazzi tailing us that night—I didn't think Isabella's spells extended quite that far—but over dinner, Max had told me Courtney had carefully leaked the news that he'd be going to a gala art gallery opening that night. The gallery was miles away in West Hollywood, and so, it seemed, were the celebrity photographers who'd made our lives miserable for the past five months.

"She does that all the time," he'd said. "Or at least, she asks one of her P.A. friends to do it for her, since that news coming straight from her would be kind of suspect. And she does the same for them."

"Sounds like you've got a real operation going," I'd remarked, and he'd only smiled.

"You gotta do what you gotta do, right?"

Now I could only be glad of the utter absence of paparazzi, and that most people had apparently decided it was a little too chilly on the beach to take a walk after dinner. Max and I had this one stretch completely to ourselves, and I could feel the tight knot of worry that seemed to have taken up permanent residence at the back of my neck begin to loosen a little.

"I could get used to this," I said, and his hand crept into mine, warm and strong despite the chill ocean breeze blowing past us.

"You want to become an L.A. girl?" he asked, a smile touching the corners of his lips, and I shook my head.

"Not really. But I can see the appeal in escaping here from time to time."

He was silent for a moment, the only sound the soft crash of the waves on the shore, the sighing of the wind in my ears. Off in the distance was the inevitable Southern California drone of cars going by, but they were far enough away that I could effectively ignore them.

"Well," he said, "how would you feel about me selling the Bel-Air house and getting something on the beach?"

Right now, that prospect sounded absolutely heavenly. Except....

"I think I'd want a place where we wouldn't need walkie-talkies to keep in touch with each other."

He chuckled. "I can manage that. Actually, I

know we'd have to downsize a little, because a house on the beach that's as big as the Bel-Air place would be almost double the price. You okay with squeezing into something that's only around four thousand square feet?"

I just had to laugh in return. "I think I can manage that."

"Then I'll have Courtney get in touch with my real estate agent, see what's available."

That was Max, always charging in even though it might have been better to hold off and wait a while. I tightened my fingers on his and said, "I think it can wait a little. After all...."

The words floated on the cool, salt-scented breeze. It was fine and good to talk about our future, to build our castles in the air, but unless we were able to exonerate Christian somehow, that future would never come to pass.

"Okay," Max said, his tone firm, "we'll start working on the real estate stuff after our honeymoon. I don't want anything to distract us while we're off having fun."

And that, too, was the man I loved—willing to admit that the present might have its share of bumps in the road, but never giving up on his vision of what he wanted.

"Sure," I said, hoping I sounded as confident as he did, "we'll do that after the honeymoon."

...if it happened at all.

CHAPTER 10

A Fitting Introduction

We slept in each other's arms that night in the huge main suite at the Bel-Air house, and were up and moving early the next morning, ready to get on Max's plane and fly back to Las Vegas. Although we'd kissed each other good night, we hadn't made love—mostly because it felt strange to be intimate with him when Courtney was sleeping under the same roof. True, the little suite she'd put together out of two spare bedrooms was at the exact opposite end of the house and I doubted she would have heard anything, but still. While there was always either Lou or Al keeping watch at the ranch, they were generally outdoors, and neither one of them slept at the property.

In fact, the door to Courtney's room was still closed when we slipped out. I worried a little about that, but Max assured me it was okay for him to leave the Porsche at the airport—Courtney had the extra key and could just get an Uber to take her over there, where she could pick up the car at her convenience.

That was why we were wheels up and in the sky by eight-thirty, even after stopping at a dive-y drive-through that had some of the best breakfast burritos I'd ever eaten.

"Nathan was right about one thing," I remarked once we were in the sky and flying east, and Max lifted an eyebrow.

"What's that?"

"I need to stop eating like this, or I'm never going to fit in that wedding gown."

He made a sound that was halfway between a laugh and a snort, telling me he didn't believe my comment for one second. And I probably was exaggerating—I had been blessed with one of those awesome metabolisms that allowed me to eat pretty much whatever I wanted and stay my same slender self, so I would have had to be eating half a dozen breakfast burritos every day to really start worrying about squeezing into the simple strapless gown I'd selected.

"What next?" I asked, and his expression abruptly sobered.

"I really don't know," he replied. "Jana obviously had nothing to do with Nathan's death, and I haven't heard a peep out of Lou. He's probably still trying to find out what he can about Todd Anderson, but...."

Max didn't finish the sentence; he didn't have to. We both knew that unless we came up with a viable alternate suspect to Christian Petrucci, nothing else much mattered.

All the same, we both tried to stay cheerful during our flight home, this time mixing things up a bit by stopping in Winslow to refuel rather than Flagstaff, and eating at one of the kitschy diners on the main drag there. We couldn't quite avoid the startled stares and requests for photos that seemed to inevitably occur whenever Max showed up in a new location, but at least people were polite...and at least we didn't have to worry about any paparazzi showing up in that isolated, dusty desert town.

Then it was time for the final leg of our journey, and we touched down in the airport outside Las Vegas a little before four that afternoon. By that time, I was more than happy to get out of the plane, although I had to admit there was something magical about being able to fly like this, about not having to worry about airports and schedules and TSA bag requirements. Max's Bronco was exactly where he'd left it, so after we'd gotten our luggage out of the Cessna, we were on our way to the ranch soon enough.

Gordon Shaw waved us through the gate, telling me Lou must be up at the house, while Al probably had the afternoon off. They probably didn't need this much coverage with Max and me out of town, but I supposed they wanted to make sure the ranch wasn't left empty while the two of us were off in California.

In fact, Lou was mixing some pizza dough as we walked into the kitchen. He paused, his floury hands resting on top of the white mass on its marble board, and said, "Perfect timing. I've got some news for you."

Good news, I hoped.

"What is it?" Max asked, slipping his overnight bag to the floor.

I did the same, since it looked like we might be in here for a while.

"That Todd Anderson guy," Lou replied. "Looks like he's got a solid alibi. He was at work all week, and Friday night, he took his wife out for dinner. Got the credit card receipts to prove it and everything."

I didn't ask how Lou had gotten access to those receipts. The man seemed to have an almost preternatural talent for digging up information from all kinds of unlikely sources.

Max's strong brown brows drew together, telling me he didn't seem too happy with this news. "Still," he said slowly, as though trying to puzzle through the situation and come up with a solution that would work for all of us, "even if Todd

Anderson took his wife out to dinner on Friday night, conceivably, he could have traveled to Las Vegas after that and done the deed. After all, we don't know when Nathan's time of death actually was. It could have been really early in the morning, like right before dawn."

Lou sent me an unreadable look, although I had a pretty good idea what he was thinking. When he spoke, I could tell he was trying to be polite.

"I don't think that's very likely," he said. "The guy's doing well for himself, but he's not the kind of person who can afford to charter a jet to do that kind of thing, and it would be hard to accomplish using only commercial flights. He'd have to go from Ontario International to Phoenix, then pick a connecting flight to Albuquerque, since no one flies direct there. And then he'd still have to drive from Albuquerque to Las Vegas."

He didn't bother to add that the drive to our little corner of the world would take the greater part of two and a half hours, since we all knew that already. Unless the guy had the teleportation talents of some of the Petruccis—which he obviously didn't—he would never have been able to manage such a feat.

"Then we're back to square one," Max said, now sounding dejected. "Because the Jana Donalds angle was a bust, too."

I reached over and gave his hand a reassuring

squeeze. "We'll figure something out," I told him. "But for now, we just need to rest—and enjoy that pizza when it's ready."

"Dinner at six-thirty," Lou informed me, looking relieved that Max wasn't going to argue the point about Todd Anderson somehow being able to magically travel to Las Vegas in the dead of night to do his terrible deed.

No, we took our bags into the bedroom, unpacked, and did our best to settle in. Or rather, while I left Max scrolling through Zillow and looking at multimillion-dollar beachfront properties in Malibu—so much for his claim that he wouldn't worry about house-hunting until we got back from our honeymoon—I decided it was time to explore my own methods of information-gathering.

Namely, tea-leaf reading.

Max had given me one of the spare bedrooms as my office, so that was where I retreated after I'd boiled some water and poured it over the gunpowder green tea in the antique cup I always used for this method of divination. While my new office wasn't quite the same as being able to settle down at the kitchen table at my old place, I had to admit it was still lovely, with its tall windows that looked out on the rolling hills to the rear of the house, and the warm wood floors and white-washed pine furniture.

I sat down at the small round table I'd placed by the window, and slowly drank the tea sip by sip, letting my thoughts linger on the question that had roiled my existence for the past couple of days.

Who really killed Nathan O'Rourke?

Once the tea was all drunk, I tipped the cup upside down so the last few drops of liquid ran onto the matching saucer, then peered inside so I could see what—if any—patterns had been left behind.

Most of the leaves had been left in a clump at the bottom of the cup, but there were two pieces stuck to one side, in slender shapes that seemed to mirror one another.

I stared at the shapes. They really didn't look like anything in particular.

A fence, maybe?

That didn't make much sense, but I couldn't think what else the shapes might be.

What did a fence mean?

Hurdles, sometimes. And sometimes it meant success after overcoming obstacles.

Well, I'd definitely like to believe that, wanted to think that somehow Max and I would get past this whole mess and still have our happily ever after. Unfortunately, the pattern the leaves had left behind didn't seem to offer anything to help me solve this mystery.

Frowning, I peered down at the wet leaves clustered at the bottom of the teacup, but there definitely weren't any discernible shapes there. Just a bunch of residue and nothing more.

Well, so much for that.

I tried to remind myself that often the meaning of the leaves became clear to me much later on, sometimes hours or even days after a reading, and I needed to be patient with myself. However, patience wasn't going to help me here, not with the wedding—and Isabella's ultimatum—less than a week away.

Holding back a curse, I picked up the cup and headed into the kitchen so I could rinse it out.

It definitely didn't seem as if I was going to find any answers today.

THE FITTING AT THE BRIDAL SHOP IN Santa Fe should have been uneventful. However, Deanne and Darcy and I had only been there for about five minutes—with Deanne already in the process of having her sky-blue bridesmaid's gown pinned in various strategic places—when my mother walked in, a girl who looked around five or six years younger than me a pace or so behind her.

"I'm so sorry," my mother said, wearing the kind of smile that told me she knew she was impinging horribly but was going to balls her way through this anyway, "but Lucy was just dying to see you, and I knew you'd be here in Santa Fe today."

"'Lucy'?" I repeated with a blink, even though I guessed she must be referring to the dark-haired young woman who now stood next to her.

And even though Alicia hadn't gotten to that part of the introductions yet, I knew exactly who Lucy must be, since she had my same dark hair and eyes, the same longish nose and full mouth.

My half-sister, the daughter Alicia'd had when she went back to New York and married the man the elders had decreed would be her spouse. However, since Lucy was so much younger than I was, it seemed as though Alicia had waited a good while before she got her second, witchy family started.

"Hi," the girl said, and came forward and gave me an unexpected and not completely welcome hug. "I know it's kind of butting in, but I really wanted to meet you—and I wanted to see Santa Fe, too. I've never been here...never been anywhere, really."

"That's a slight exaggeration," Alicia remarked, although she wore a fond smile as she looked at her daughter...the kind of look she'd never given me during her brief visit a year ago. "We travel a good bit, but I have to admit we've never made it to this part of the country."

Of course not. Alicia would have had to do everything she could to prevent her daughter from meeting me, since she'd been doing her best to keep my existence a secret. But with the cat out of the bag now, she probably figured it was a good time to introduce us.

I might have had a few choice words to say to her on that subject, since dumping a half-sister on me when I was in the final sprint toward a wedding ceremony and trying to solve a murder at the same time wasn't the kindest thing in the world, but I'd never thought Alicia was exactly overbrimming with tact.

"Well, Santa Fe is kind of special," I said, figuring I might as well attempt to be diplomatic. "So I can see why you'd want to come. And it's fine —I'm glad to meet you, Lucy. Just don't whisper a word to Max about what my wedding gown looks like."

At the mention of my future husband, Lucy's expression turned positively dreamy. "It's *so* romantic," she gushed. "Marrying the boy next door, who turns out to be a movie star? Nothing like that *ever* happens in my family."

Of course it didn't...not with the Petrucci elders decreeing who could marry whom.

However, that wasn't the sort of thing I could exactly point out in front of an audience, even though Deanne was currently occupied with the seamstress and Darcy had wandered over to the racks of wedding gowns and was looking through them while waiting for her turn to get pinned and prodded. I hadn't heard that Darcy was dating anyone in particular, and guessed her current interest had more to do with wasting time than because she was planning her own wedding.

Still, since it seemed better to be discreet until I could talk to Alicia and Lucy in private—if that even happened at all—I only cleared my throat and said, "Yes, I think it's pretty romantic, too. Are you going to stay for the wedding? Because I'm sure Max and I can find a few extra places at the reception for you and your mom."

Those words just sort of came out in a blurt, and weren't anything I'd been planning. But because I knew it would seem kind of strange to have my long-lost mother and half-sister in town and not invite them to the wedding, I couldn't stop myself from making the offer.

Surprise flared in my mother's eyes, although I could tell she was doing her best to hide how startled she was by the invitation. Before she could say anything, though, Lucy replied, "Oh, really? That would be wonderful!"

"Yes, I'd really like to have you there," I said. "I can get you a formal invitation later, since that will have all the details on it."

"That's very kind of you, Skye," Alicia said,

and although the air felt heavy with all the things she might have liked to add, I could tell she was holding back because we weren't alone.

Lucy, on the other hand, appeared all enthusiasm. "Sounds like I need to go shopping—and Santa Fe seems like the perfect place to do it. Be back in a bit!"

And she practically danced out of the store, clearly intent on doing some serious damage to her credit cards.

Or maybe they were Alicia's credit cards. I honestly didn't know what their domestic setup was like, and whether Lucy was out on her own or not. Twenty-four was definitely old enough for her to have set up her own household, but then again, New York was an expensive place to live.

Alicia wore a smile that bordered on indulgent, although I couldn't read much more of her expression than that. "Lucy does love shopping," she said, then paused, casting a glance toward the spot a few yards away where Deanne was getting more pins stuck into her. My friend's eyes were full of questions, but clearly, she was glued onto that dais until the seamstress let her know she was finished adjusting her gown. After apparently reassuring herself that no one could overhear what we were saying, Alicia added in a low tone, "Thank you again for the invitation...even though I'm afraid it might be a little premature."

"You don't think Max and I can figure out who killed Nathan O'Rourke?" I asked, knowing the note in my voice might have been a little too challenging.

"I wouldn't presume," Alicia replied serenely. "After all, I've seen you in action before. I'm just saying that Isabella isn't going to back down if you're unable to find the murderer."

"Believe me, I know," I said. "And I'm doing whatever I can to get this whole mess sorted out." I paused there, then inquired, "I'm just surprised you didn't mention that Lucy had come with you to New Mexico. You didn't say anything when we were all at the Plaza the other day."

Once again, Alicia's gaze shifted toward Deanne, but although it looked as if the seamstress was winding down, I guessed my friend wouldn't be freed from her bridesmaid's gown and sent off to change back into her street clothes for at least a couple more minutes.

"Because Lucy didn't come with me," Alicia explained. "She decided this morning to drop in after I told her I wasn't sure when I was going to be back in New York. She wanted to see the half-sister she'd never met, and didn't much care that you had a lot going on."

Although I'd only just met Lucy, my mother's explanation jibed with my initial impression of my half-sister. She did what she wanted, and everyone else needed to stand back. However....

"She decided this morning?" I asked. "How did she get here so quickly?'

Alicia's mouth twitched. "My daughter inherited the Petrucci gift for teleporting...something I was never very good at. But Lucy comes and goes as she pleases, and since she's also very skilled with invisibility, she can pop in anywhere she likes."

Handy. Max and I could have saved ourselves a lot of time if I had that particular skill. Then again, I really didn't know whether I had it or not. I hadn't practiced using my Petrucci magic, had done the best I could to pretend I didn't have it at all, so I really had no idea whether I was able to send myself thousands of miles in a blink or not.

Honestly, it wasn't the sort of magic I wanted to practice. It had the potential to go horribly, horribly wrong.

A stray thought moved through my brain, one I wasn't sure I wanted to acknowledge.

Being able to pop in and out of existence like that would be awfully handy if you wanted to commit a crime...say, a murder.

I told myself that was ridiculous, that Lucy Petrucci would have absolutely no reason in the world to kill Nathan O'Rourke. Even if she had, she was so slim, it looked like even I could have broken her over my knee. There was no way she could have been responsible for the kind of physical mayhem the paparazzo had suffered.

So, of course she couldn't be the one responsible for Nathan's death...but that didn't mean someone else in her witch family might be equally innocent. What if Carmela, who seemed to be the one of the three elders who was particularly good at teleporting, had decided to off Nathan, for whatever reason?

No, that didn't make sense. Killing Nathan had turned police scrutiny on Christian, which you'd think was the last thing any of the Petruccis would want.

Unless they'd done so specifically to force the timeline, to get me to marry him before he was sent down the river for the next twenty or thirty years.

I really couldn't wrap my brain around that kind of twisted thinking, but then again, the Petruccis had done a lot of things over the years that didn't make much sense on the surface.

Still, I thought I'd better back-burner that particular theory until I could discuss it in person with Max.

"That must save on plane tickets and hotel rooms," I joked feebly, but Alicia didn't smile.

"Oh, she still likes hotels," she said. "In fact, Lucy's staying at the Castañeda—the Plaza didn't have any more rooms left, since so many people are coming in from out of town for your wedding." A pause, and then Alicia added, "I know we've already inserted ourselves in your wedding, but would you mind too much if we invited my son Luke as well? It would seem strange not to have both your half-siblings there."

Luke and Lucy? I wasn't sure what to think about that, although I supposed it was slightly better than naming them Luke and Leia.

As for the rest of her request, the more, the merrier. Andie and I had already decided to include food for an extra five people as part of the catering package, just because we thought it would be safer in order to accommodate any last-minute additions. Now I'd already filled up three of those five slots, and would just have to cross my fingers that no more long-lost relatives were going to show up out of the blue.

"Absolutely," I said. "I'd love to meet Luke." I paused there, wondering whether I should ask or not. Then again, if yet another person was going to be added to the guest list, the further ahead I knew, the better. "Is he married? Because I'm sure we can squeeze another person in. I just need to know in advance."

The faintest line appeared between Alicia's arched, dark brows. I'd seen that happen before, and recalled it was a sign she was troubled about something, even if she didn't want to admit it openly.

"He is married," she said calmly. "But he and Cora have been having a little trouble lately. I think it's probably best if he comes by himself."

So much for those "happy" arranged marriages, I thought. I knew better than to say such a thing out loud, though, so I only responded, "Oh, I'm sorry to hear that."

"I'm sure it will work itself out," Alicia said, still in that too-serene tone. "Newlywed friction, that's all it is."

Somehow, I got the feeling it was more than that, but I certainly wasn't going to ask any probing questions. It was none of my business, and besides, I guessed that Alicia wouldn't appreciate me prying into her son's affairs. Really, it didn't seem too odd that a couple of people who'd been basically forced to marry each other weren't having the best of times.

If that was even what was going on at all. Maybe sometimes Petruccis had the good luck to fall in love with safely distant cousins, and therefore didn't need the elders sticking their noses in where they didn't belong.

Or maybe I was being entirely too optimistic about the situation.

Either way, I didn't have much time to brood on the problem, because Deanne, now done with her fitting and back in her regular clothes, came over to the spot where I was standing with Alicia. I could tell my friend was having a hard time maintaining a pleasant expression—she'd been even angrier with Alicia than I was when my long-lost mother bailed on me last year—but was doing her best to be nice for my sake.

"Oh, hi, Alicia," Deanne said, in the sort of falsely bright tone that usually seemed reserved for kindergarten teachers and telemarketers. "This is a nice surprise."

"I didn't want to miss Skye's big day," Alicia replied, appearing to go with the flow. "And she's very kindly invited me and her half-brother and -sister to the wedding."

Deanne's eyes widened and she sent me a sideways glance that seemed to indicate she thought I'd lost my mind. But she sounded friendly enough as she said, "Oh, was that who that girl was? Skye's sister?"

"Lucy," I supplied. "She was very excited to find out she'd been invited to the wedding, so she went off to shop for something special to wear. You'd think she'd been invited to the Oscars or something."

Since Deanne had a love of shopping that dinky little Las Vegas could never satisfy, I hoped she'd find Lucy's actions endearing rather than impetuous. And that seemed to be the case, because my friend's posture grew a little less tense as she said, "Oh, that sounds like fun. This is a great place for shopping. I got Skye the prettiest sweater a couple of years ago—"

And they were off and running, talking about the shopping in downtown Santa Fe and which boutiques had the best selection and prices. It all seemed completely normal, even if I knew the situation was anything but.

Still, I welcomed the utter mundanity of their conversation. I wanted the whole rest of the week to be like that—just the sort of busywork you always had to deal with when leading up to a wedding, no interfering witch elders or arranged marriages...or dead bodies.

Unfortunately, I had a feeling my wishes on that particular subject had no intention of coming true.

CHAPTER 11

Sleight of Hand

"You think Carmela killed Nathan O'Rourke?" Max asked, looking startled.

I'd returned from my trip to Santa Fe about half an hour earlier, getting home a little before six. Deanne and Darcy had made some noises about wanting to stay in Santa Fe and have an early dinner, but I'd told them I was tired and just wanted to head back to Las Vegas. Luckily, the bride's wishes trumped everything else, and since Alicia and Lucy had already left—the latter sporting several large bags of new clothes—my friends hadn't argued.

And both Darcy and Deanne studiously avoided commenting on the unexpected appearance of my mother and the half-sister I'd never met before now, both of them seeming to understand it was a sore topic for me and that I didn't want to discuss it. To be perfectly honest, I wasn't sure exactly how I was supposed to feel about the entire situation. Alicia had revealed to me when she was in New Mexico the year before that I had a pair of half-siblings, but she hadn't provided any real details and I hadn't pushed. I hadn't thought I would ever meet them, so it hadn't seemed useful to dwell on the reality of their existence, or to wonder what they were like, or if we resembled one another at all.

Well, Lucy's appearance today had proven that one particular point; we looked a lot alike, although she was more olive-skinned, like our mother, and not quite as tall as I was. It didn't seem as if she'd inherited much from her father in terms of her appearance, which was the case with me as well. I really didn't look anything like the O'Malley side of the family, even if theirs was the name I bore.

At any rate, I'd told Max about how Alicia and Lucy had shown up at the bridal shop, and how I'd invited them—and my half-brother Luke—to the wedding. Max had taken all of this in stride... mostly...but after I shoved the subject of their unexpected arrival aside, it seemed I'd really pushed the limit with my suspicions about Carmela.

"Well, why not?" I asked. "She can teleport anywhere she wants, and I'm sure a witch would be pretty good at erasing evidence, too. Is it so crazy that she'd be angry about Nathan's threats, and decided to get rid of him and his lawsuits permanently before he invited any scrutiny of the Petrucci family?"

For a moment, Max didn't reply. We were sitting in the family room, with the windows open to let in a fresh breeze off the hillsides beyond the patio, but neither of us had relaxed very much into our environment. Part of that was probably because he'd told Lou to take the night off, and we were about to head into town to get dinner at Smoky Joe's—I wasn't sure when I'd feel comfortable showing my face at The Skillet again—but I guessed it was more that neither of us really wanted to be talking about any of this, even though we knew we needed to do it now when we had some privacy.

"I'm not saying it's crazy," Max replied. "I guess I'm just trying to visualize the whole thing. The police said someone had basically hit him upside the head with a baseball bat or something, right?"

That description made me wince. "I'm not sure they were that specific. They just said he was beaten and died from his injuries. If I were at Levitation Latte today, I might've had a chance to talk to Kyle and see what he knows. But with the shop closed for the next three weeks, I'm not going to have any time to talk to him and get the details."

I hadn't meant any criticism of Max's encouragement to close up things for the coming week, but he frowned anyway. "You don't really think you could've handled all this and worked at the store, do you?"

At once, I reached over and placed my hand on his. "No, of course not. That's not what I meant at all. But now it's going to be a lot harder to pick Kyle's brain."

Max didn't look too fazed by this complication. "Not really. Just call him and ask him to come over."

I raised an eyebrow. "I thought we were going out to eat."

"We were," Max said easily. "But I can get us a bunch of takeout. See if he's available, and I'll call in an order to Smoky Joe's."

He made it all sound so easy. True, Kyle and I were on much better terms now that he seemed to have finally accepted the reality that my relationship with Max wasn't going anywhere, but still, it was one thing to have a casual gossip when dropping into a coffee shop, and something else entirely to go over to someone's house for dinner.

But, as Max had pointed out, this seemed like the best way to get some inside information on the case. I sure as hell couldn't walk into Marie DeVargas's office and ask her to give me the coroner's report, pretty please?

That seemed to decide things. I reached for my

purse, which I had sitting on the coffee table in preparation for our departure to get dinner, and pulled out my iPhone.

Although I didn't call him very often, I still had Kyle's number stored in my contacts list. No matter what, he was going to think it strange that I was reaching out to him now, but I couldn't worry about that, not when he was the only person who might be able to help answer some questions tonight. Darcy also worked at the police station, but she'd already told me she was pulling a night shift this evening, part of the reason why she'd been able to come to Santa Fe with Deanne and me earlier today.

Now I just had to hope Kyle wasn't working, too. Mostly, he seemed to get day shifts, maybe because he had more seniority than some of the other deputies and therefore got a better schedule most of the time.

Kyle picked up right away, telling me he probably wasn't on duty. "Skye?" he said, sounding surprised. "What's up?"

"You doing anything tonight?" I asked, and although I couldn't see his expression, I had to believe his forehead had scrunched in puzzlement after hearing my question.

"Um...no," he replied, his tone guarded. "Why?"

"Max and I are getting some takeout from

Smoky Joe's and were wondering if you'd like to come over."

A short silence. Then Kyle said, "Um...okay. What time?"

"Six-thirty?" I responded. It was now a little past six, and we still had to place the order and have Max go into town to pick it up.

"Sure...see you then."

He still sounded sort of mystified, and I couldn't really blame him. The important thing, though, was that he'd agreed to come over.

Our call ended, I set the phone down on the coffee table and turned toward Max.

"Okay," I said. "We're set. Now we just have to hope Kyle has some good information for us."

MAX GOT HOME A BARE TWO MINUTES before Kyle showed up. In a way, that was a good thing, because we wouldn't have to worry about the food sitting for a while in the kitchen on top of having to survive the trip back to the ranch. And since I'd set the table while Max was running his errand, we were ready to sit down almost at once.

"Thanks for coming," I said as we handed around bowls of smoked brisket and mac and cheese and salad. "We were hoping we could pick your brain a little."

Kyle, who'd just dumped a heaping spoonful of Smoky Joe's famous green chile mac and cheese on his plate, shot me a sideways smile. "I kind of figured it was something like that. We haven't had much of a chance to talk lately."

"No, things have been a little hectic," I agreed. Since I'd already guessed he had to know this wasn't merely a social visit, I didn't see the point in trying to hide the real reason why we'd invited him out here this evening.

Max took a bite of brisket, then said, "Can you fill us in on any of the details about Nathan O'Rourke's murder?"

Straight and to the point. Luckily, Kyle didn't seem too put out by the question...although we had to wait for him to finish chewing the mouthful of mac and cheese he'd just lifted to his lips.

"Sure," he said, then added, "on one condition."

"What's that?" I asked, hoping it wouldn't be anything too crazy, like telling me I had to cancel the wedding or promise the entire Las Vegas police force free muffins and coffee for the rest of my life.

Now looking sheepish, Kyle said, "Can you set up something where I'd get to see Andie again? She seems really nice, and...."

He didn't finish the sentence, probably because his face had flamed bright red as he made the request and he didn't want to dig himself in any deeper than he already had.

Since I'd already noticed he was interested in her...and she seemed to possibly be interested in him...I was perfectly happy to fill that request.

"Sure," I said. "I'm meeting with her again on Wednesday afternoon at the hotel ballroom. We'll be there at three-thirty, so just figure out a reason to drop by right then—maybe say you're performing a safety inspection or something."

Now even the tips of Kyle's ears looked red, but he managed to say in an almost casual tone, "Okay, that'll work. I'm on duty that afternoon, so it'll be easy enough to swing by."

"Good," Max put in. "Now that we've got that settled, what about Nathan O'Rourke's murder?"

Kyle reached for the glass of wine at his place setting and took a sip. "I'll tell you what I know, which isn't all that much. We're pretty sure the time of death was sometime between two and three in the morning, and, judging by the lack of physical evidence in his vehicle, it looks like he was killed somewhere else and then left in his Jeep. Unfortunately, we haven't been able to locate the exact spot where the crime occurred."

Well, that didn't seem too implausible. Even though Las Vegas itself wasn't that big, there was plenty of open land all around, and lots of isolated places where you could carry out all kinds of mayhem undetected. Unless the local police decided to go over every square inch of land spanning thousands of acres—and they definitely didn't have the resources for that—I didn't know whether they'd ever be able to pinpoint the place where Nathan O'Rourke had met his end.

"Any evidence on the body that might point toward a killer?" I asked then. "Maybe a hair that wasn't his, cloth fibers, anything like that?"

Kyle shook his head, although he also looked almost grimly amused, as though he knew the Skye O'Malley of a couple of years ago wouldn't have even known to ask questions like that.

"Nothing," he said, and swallowed some more wine. "Whoever killed him seemed to have taken a lot of precautions."

"Do you think a woman could have done it?" I said, and he gave me a startled look.

"What, do you know something about an angry ex-girlfriend that we don't?"

"No," I replied hastily, even as I thought of Jana Donalds, sitting alone in her multi-million-dollar mansion, trying to ignore her grief at learning the man she'd once cared for had died violently. "I'm just trying to figure out whether there's any possibility, or whether it had to have been a man."

Kyle pushed around some of the mac and cheese on his plate, as if doing so might help him focus on the matter at hand. "I honestly don't know," he said at length. "I mean, the guy's head was bashed in, so you wouldn't think a woman would have the strength to do something like that. But people do all kinds of crazy things in the heat of the moment. I can't really say one way or another, but it seems pretty unlikely to me."

Well, that wasn't the definitive answer I'd been looking for, and yet it did seem as though whoever had murdered Nathan O'Rourke had been angry enough to commit some pretty serious physical mayhem. Just the thought of leaving this earth by way of such an act of violence made me shiver, and I reached for my glass of wine so I could take a much-needed sip.

"Any idea what the weapon was?" Max inquired. If he was feeling at all squeamish at hearing exactly how Nathan had met his end, he didn't show it.

"Some kind of blunt object," Kyle replied. "Maybe a baseball bat or a mallet. We're pretty sure it wasn't a hammer, because something like that would have inflicted a lot more open wounds."

Yikes. Suddenly, the food on my plate didn't seem quite so appetizing, and I swallowed some more wine.

Max, obviously made of sterner stuff, helped himself to a bite of brisket, then said, "Either way, it's not the kind of weapon that could be easily traced."

"Nope," Kyle agreed around a bite of cornbread. "And we've checked with the local hardware stores and at Walmart, and no one remembers anyone buying that kind of stuff recently—at least, no one who stands out. Sure, there were people buying their kids baseball bats because Little League practice just started up again, but no strangers, no one who would've had a grudge against Nathan O'Rourke."

Well, it sure sounded as though the Las Vegas P.D. had been covering all the bases...so to speak. And while all this had been interesting, I wasn't sure if any of it was really going to help in the long run.

Max, however, seemed undeterred. "So, it sounds to me as though someone must have come here from out of town with murder on their mind, and brought the weapon with them."

"It seems that way," Kyle replied. "And even though this isn't tourist season, we still have enough strangers in town that it would be hard to pin this on any one person, especially if they came in, killed O'Rourke, and then left immediately afterward."

Great. This was all sounding better and better. Not that I really expected the Las Vegas police to have narrowed the case down to one suspect so quickly, but I supposed I'd still hoped they might have some theories.

Unfortunately, they sounded just as flummoxed as I was...and that meant Max and I were no closer to discovering who really had taken that baseball bat to Nathan O'Rourke's skull...or why.

At least no one except Max and I—and the Petrucci witches, of course—knew anything about the terrible bargain I'd made with Isabella. To Kyle...and to Deanne and anyone else...this only looked like me embarking on yet another of my investigations, one that didn't have any real personal stakes.

If only they knew.

For one moment, my gaze met Max's clear blue eyes. He looked undaunted, but a certain tension to his neck and jaw told me he wasn't happy that Kyle hadn't been able to provide any useful information.

"Well," I said lightly, "it sucks for the investigation, but I suppose it's something to know that at least the killer isn't hanging around town, looking for his latest victim."

Kyle chuckled a little, but there wasn't much humor in the sound. "Nope, nothing like that. We tried checking to see who out there might have had a grudge against him, but nothing really panned out. It seems like he was the kind of guy who didn't have a lot of friends and had a bunch of people who didn't like him very much, but nobody seemed to dislike him enough to murder him. I can't say I disagree with those people who didn't care for him, because he seemed like kind of a jerk."

Oh, Nathan O'Rourke was definitely a very big jerk. Still, jerkdom wasn't a good enough reason for clocking someone in the head with a baseball bat.

"If it's any consolation," Kyle went on, "I don't think your cousin did it. He has a really crappy alibi, but he doesn't seem like a killer."

"Think you could tell the D.A. that, maybe see if he'll drop the charges?" I asked, only half-joking.

Kyle shook his head. "I wish I had that kind of clout. But because a bunch of witnesses saw your cousin sock Nathan in the jaw, it just follows that he might be capable of the kind of violence that took the guy's life later that night." He broke off a piece of cornbread, put it in his mouth and chewed, then said, "If it's any consolation, I'm sure a jury will see it the same way. You just have to hang tight and let the justice system do its job."

Under different circumstances, I might have agreed. But Isabella didn't seem to have the same confidence that Christian would be vindicated, and therefore wanted to make sure he was married and a new little Petrucci baby on the way before the trial even began.

And with no real evidence and no more clues

to go on, I really didn't know what I was supposed to do next.

Giving up wasn't an option, though, so I'd just have to muddle through and hope something useful would present itself.

"In the meantime, though, I think we'll keep poking around," Max said. "It couldn't hurt, right?"

"No," Kyle responded. "As long as you're not too obvious about it. Chief DeVargas would be pissed if something you did messed up a piece of evidence, or whatever."

"We'll be careful," I promised. "And honestly, we're not even sure where to go next with this, so we'll just have to kind of wait and see what happens."

Kyle must have seen the dejected expression on my face, because he said, "If anything new comes up, I'll definitely let you know about it. I mean, it's got to suck having this hanging over your cousin's head with your wedding only a few days away."

You have no idea, I thought. And that was a good thing. No one except the parties involved should have to know anything about the kind of future I was facing if we didn't get this murder resolved in the next couple of days.

I made some kind of sound of assent, and the conversation moved on to less fraught topics, like the warm weather we'd been having and the possibility of a decent monsoon season this summer. Once we were done with dinner and Kyle was on his way back to town, I began to pick up our dishes...and sent Max a despairing look.

"What're we supposed to do now?" I asked plaintively, and he came over and took the plates from my hands so he could put his arms around my waist.

"The same thing you always do," he replied without hesitation. "Find your way through despite everything. It's going to be okay."

I wasn't so sure about that, but somehow, it was hard to feel too worried with Max holding me like that, the whisper of his cologne a welcome fragrance, every inch of his body strong and sturdy and reassuring. How could things go wrong when I had him in my life?

They already have, my brain told me.

They already have.

CHAPTER 12

Matchmaking

But one thing I knew about bad times—like when my grandmother died and I truly thought I was alone in this world, even though I knew I had friends who cared about me—was that you still had to get through them, no matter what. That meant meeting with Andie on Tuesday and going over the minutiae of the reception...how I wanted the bows on the backs of the chairs tied, which song the band needed to play for my first dance with Max...and then sitting down for an interview at the ranch with a reporter from *People* magazine, and talking about the wedding and our upcoming honeymoon. The piece wouldn't be published until well after the big day, and I had to hope they'd have time to stop the presses in case we couldn't come up with a murderer and I was forced to marry Christian after all.

I think we both sounded normal, or at least, Max was a consummate actor and did a great job of hiding the stress we were both under, and I did my best to follow his lead, to act as though everything was completely normal and I didn't have anything to worry about except making sure the flowers arrived on schedule and that our security team would do an adequate job of keeping the photographers far away from the Ilfeld Ballroom.

We had a quiet dinner at home, watched some TV, and then went to bed, Max as usual holding me in his arms as we both fell asleep.

And then I dreamed.

I couldn't always tell which were my "true" dreams and which ones were just the usual subconscious mishmash of the activities and conversations my brain had processed that day, but something about this one seemed to signal I needed to pay particular attention.

The scene in my head was a nighttime one, the details blurry, indistinct. All the same, I thought I saw someone push a man out of a vehicle, a gray sedan of some kind, although I couldn't make out any logos or details that would have told me the model. Little puffs of dust came out from the dry ground where the man fell, but he didn't move.

Someone else got out of the vehicle, someone in jeans and a black shirt, although I couldn't see any more details than that. Then they lifted something dark and blunt in their hands and brought it down on the man's head, beating him several times before finally taking the thing they held—bat, mallet, I couldn't be sure—and hurling it far out into the wilderness, into the dark.

At the very last minute, right before they moved to get into the car, the person turned and stared in the direction where I would have been standing if I'd actually been there.

Dark eyes met mine.

The person in my dream was me.

No, my brain corrected itself. *Not me.*

My half-sister, Lucy Petrucci.

I gasped and sat up, and at once Max reached out to put a comforting hand on my arm.

"Are you okay?"

"Fine," I managed, although I knew I sounded breathless, not quite myself. "I had a dream."

"A real dream?" he asked, then pushed himself up on his elbows. In the faint light from the clock radio on my side of the bed, his expression was hard to read clearly, but I thought he looked excited. "About Nathan?"

"I think so," I said, and made myself pause for a moment there, my brain doing its best to lock onto the details from the dream before they faded from my memory. "I couldn't see his face clearly. But I saw the killer."

"You did?" Max's fingers tightened on my arm,

not nearly enough to hurt, but definitely enough to signal how excited he was.

"Yes," I said, and pulled in a breath. "Max, it was my half-sister."

At that revelation, he let go of my arm and stared at me in consternation. "Your *sister?*"

I nodded. "I know it sounds crazy. But I saw her face—and I saw the car she was driving. I couldn't tell exactly what it was, but it was big and gray...just like Alicia's BMW."

Brows drawing together, he said, "You made it sound as if all the Petruccis teleported here, like your sister was good at that kind of thing. Why would she need a car?"

The words weren't accusing. No, Max was only trying to get to the heart of the matter based on the things I'd already told him. "I know," I replied. "That part doesn't make sense. Unless she couldn't handle teleporting while carrying Nathan's body?"

"But she brought your mother to Las Vegas by teleporting," Max pointed out, and I gave a helpless little shrug.

"True," I said. "Then again, it was a dream. Sometimes all the little details aren't totally accurate."

He was silent for a moment, then reached up to run a hand through his hair, tousling the bedhead that much more. "What do we do now?"

"I don't know," I said. "I just don't know."

THE IMAGE OF MY SISTER'S FACE STILL haunted me when I woke up the next morning. I hadn't slept well the remainder of the night, drifting in and out of consciousness, and I awoke unrefreshed and worried, not sure how I should handle the unwelcome revelation I'd seen in that terrible dream.

Should I go to the police?

No, they'd laugh me right out of the station. I might have had some good luck lately in solving crimes, but dreams weren't admissible as evidence, even if some of mine had proved to be spookily accurate.

"We'll figure it out," Max told me after we'd settled down in the family room to have some coffee. That morning, Lou wasn't there to make our early shot of caffeine, since Max had given him the day off yesterday, although I knew Al was already at his usual post at the front gate, and Gordon was probably walking the perimeter of the house, just to be safe. I assumed Lou would appear eventually, and I supposed it was a good thing we were alone right now. At least this way, we could discuss the dream without having to worry about being overheard.

"Maybe I should talk to Alicia," I suggested,

and Max tilted his head slightly, obviously considering the pros and cons of such a move.

"Do you think she'd believe you?"

"Well, I'd have more chance of that than the police thinking I was anything other than crazy," I replied. "At least she knows I inherited both her family's magic and the O'Malley magic, so it's not a question of her not believing that part of the story. I just don't know whether she'd be willing to entertain the notion that her daughter is a stone-cold killer."

In the cold light of day, I wasn't sure whether even I was willing to think such a thing. Lucy had seemed bubbly and light-hearted and fun, and not exactly the kind of person you could imagine bludgeoning a man to death.

Of course, I didn't have to imagine it. I'd seen the murder in my dream.

"Why in the world would your sister even want to kill Nathan O'Rourke?" Max asked next. "She didn't know the guy, so what possible motive could she have had?"

That was a question I knew I couldn't answer. As far as I could tell, there wouldn't have been any way for the two of them to even have interacted. Alicia had said that Lucy had come to New Mexico on Monday morning, long after Nathan was murdered. She wasn't even here the night the man died.

Or...was she? After all, Alicia herself had said that Lucy was very good at teleporting. She could have come and gone without anyone knowing she'd even been here at all.

Of course, that didn't explain the big gray car in my dream, the one that might or might not have been Alicia's BMW sedan. Not much need for a car when you could blip yourself hither and yon without even batting an eye.

Unless, of course, Nathan had been too heavy to move by means of magic, even if it sounded as though Lucy didn't have a problem transporting Alicia that same way. She probably weighed fifty pounds less than he did, or even more.

"No motive at all that I can think of," I said in reply to Max's question. "Maybe it wasn't a true dream, even if it felt like one."

Somehow, though, I knew that evaluation wasn't correct. Just because I couldn't figure out what the dream had been trying to tell me didn't mean it hadn't contained valuable information.

Problem was, none of it seemed to be remotely actionable, leaving us right where we'd started.

"No, I think it was a true dream," he said. "It'll come clear at some point. Was there anything in the dream that felt like a connection to the tea-leaf reading you did on Sunday?"

"Nothing at all," I told him, knowing I sounded utterly disgusted with the whole situation.

"The only thing I saw was a couple of sort of wavy lines, and the only thing they looked like was maybe a fence. There weren't any fences in my dream, that's for sure."

Since we were sitting next to each other, it was easy enough for him to lean over and give me a kiss on the cheek, then wrap a comforting arm around my waist. After sipping from the coffee he held in his other hand, he said, "It'll come clear in time."

"Well, it had better hurry up," I snapped. "It's Wednesday, and I've only got until Friday afternoon to get this figured out."

Against mine, his body tensed a little, but he still sounded relaxed enough as he said, "I have faith in you."

That made one of us.

I didn't say that out loud, though, because I knew I was being defeatist enough as it was. Figuring a change of subject would probably do both of us good, I ventured, "I'm really interested to see what happens with Kyle and Andie. It would be awesome for him to finally find someone special."

"Fingers crossed," Max said, then added, "I know he's still not totally mooning after you, but it would be great for someone else to distract him for a while."

"I guess we'll just have to see," I replied, and left it at that.

All the same, I was looking forward to their "accidental" meeting this afternoon. With any luck, it might help distract me a little bit from my own troubles.

———

ANDIE WAS RIGHT ON TIME, AS I'D expected. She'd brought her final layout for the reception, along with a sample of the wedding cake and several of the hors d'oeuvres. Max and I had already tasted the cake, of course, back when we were deciding what we wanted, but it seemed she wanted to make sure I hadn't changed my mind at the last minute.

"It's even better than the first time I tried it," I told her, after savoring a second mouthful of vanilla salted caramel. "People are going to go crazy for it."

Her cheeks turned a little pink. You'd think after being in the business for five-plus years and winning numerous accolades, she'd be used to that kind of praise, but apparently not.

"Thanks," she said. "It means a lot coming from you—I know what a great baker you are."

I shrugged. "I suppose I'm pretty good at muffins and pastries and that kind of stuff, but I've never attempted anything as ambitious as a wedding cake."

Well, except Deanne's. She'd begged me to do it, and I'd put together a luscious chocolate raspberry confection she was still raving about years later. All the same, it had been an enormous amount of work, and I didn't plan to do anything like that again any time soon...especially not for my own wedding.

"It's really not that hard," Andie said. "Just time-consuming. But I'm glad the cake is okay, and I'm glad you like the layout I came up with."

She glanced around the ballroom, as if sizing it up for the umpteenth time to make sure her measurements really were going to work out all right in real life. At the same time, though, I caught a certain kind of wistfulness in her expression.

Or maybe I was just reading her wrong.

"Is everything all right?" I asked. "Do you think you need to measure the room again?"

At once, she shook her head. "No, I've measured everything four times, and I know we're good to go. I guess I was just thinking about how much fun this hotel and this ballroom are, how cute your whole town is. I was born in this state, but I never had a chance to visit Las Vegas until a year ago. I kind of fell in love with it, although I knew living here probably wouldn't work for me. There's just not enough business around here to keep me going, whereas in Santa Fe, I'm booked pretty much every week."

This all sounded just about perfect to me. Andie already liked the town, and if Kyle gave her even more of a reason to stick around....

Okay, I knew that was being awfully premature, since all the two of them had done so far was exchange a couple of loaded looks. Still, a bit of wishful thinking never hurt anyone, and I figured if Max could re-order his life enough to settle down here, then it shouldn't be too difficult for Andie, if and when the time came.

"It's definitely a great place to live," I said, hoping my comment wouldn't sound too rah-rah on the subject of Las Vegas. "I mean, I like going to Santa Fe to shop and stuff, but it's always nice to come back here when I'm done."

She nodded, and looked as though she was about to say something else when Kyle entered the room.

"Oh, hi, Kyle," I said, praying I sounded casual and not at all as though this meeting had been planned. "You remember Andie, my caterer?"

"Hi, Andie," he replied. "How's the wedding planning going?"

"Just fine," she said. Once again, her cheeks looked a little pink, but she didn't seem suspicious about his presence at the hotel. "Skye and I just needed to go over a few things. I hope everything is okay here?"

She ended on a rising note, as if wanting to ask why he was at the Plaza without being too obvious.

"Oh," he said, "I came in to grab an iced tea, since Levitation Latte is closed for the duration. But then Nora at the front desk said Skye was in here, so I thought I'd just poke my head in and say hi."

All of that sounded completely reasonable to me, and apparently Andie thought the same thing as well, because she just nodded. "I know it's an inconvenience for everyone, but it's still probably a good idea that the shop is closed this week."

A better idea than even she knew, although I realized I'd better not point that out, not unless I wanted to share confidences which needed to be kept secret. "It could be worse," I said with a smile. "At least you can always get your caffeine fix here if you need to."

"Your coffee's better, though," Kyle responded. "And your pastries."

True, even if the refreshments they served at the little coffee cart in the lobby were perfectly fine. Also, I had a feeling he had to pay for those, while I'd always provided freebies whenever he stopped in at my store.

"Skye's muffins are magical, that's for sure," Andie said.

Well, I didn't know about magic, but they were definitely made with love. All the same, I had to admit I was enjoying this time off, the novel experience of having the luxury to wake up whenever I felt like it and not hours before the crack of dawn.

I knew if I wanted to, I could have this life forever. Max had already said he hoped I would be able to travel with him, and I....

You need to get this murder figured out before you start contemplating a jet-set lifestyle with Max, I told myself.

Since that was the simple truth, there wasn't much point in putting forth any further interior arguments.

"Oh, they're just muffins," I said deprecatingly. "And I've made a lot of them over the years, which is why they're decent."

"More than decent," Kyle returned, but he was smiling. "You hate compliments, though, so I guess I'll leave it there." He glanced over at Andie, and added, "It was nice to see you again, Andie. I'll see you at the wedding on Saturday."

He lifted a hand in farewell, then headed out into the lobby. Andie watched him go, and looked over at me. "Would it be awful if I asked you to seat me at his table? I know there's an empty chair at that one."

Somehow, I managed to stifle a smile. I'd told Andie she should sit down and enjoy the reception, since most of her work would be done by that point, although she still had to make sure the cake was set up in the right place and at the right time. She'd told me she didn't think that would work, that she'd still be on duty.

Now, though, it sure looked to me as if she was fine with bending that rule if it meant she could sit next to Kyle.

"No problem at all," I said serenely, even as I inwardly cheered at knowing the two of them were inching closer to a possible date.

If only I could solve my own problems so neatly.

CHAPTER 13

Clues Blues

Still, even though I hadn't gotten any closer to discovering who had killed Nathan O'Rourke—and why in the world I'd had a dream that seemed to point to my half-sister as the murderer—I couldn't help feeling cheerful as I drove home from my meeting with Andie at the ballroom. At least it seemed as though things were progressing well with her and Kyle, although I supposed I'd really have to wait and see how things went at the reception to tell if they were going to hit it off after spending more time together.

If, of course, there was a reception at all.

I also kept turning the dream over in my mind, trying to see if there was some tiny clue I'd missed, some overlooked detail that would help me interpret it correctly. No matter what I did, though, I couldn't seem to make sense of the thing.

Why in the world would Lucy have killed Nathan O'Rourke? They didn't even know each other. Also, she was just as slender as I, and a few inches shorter. She didn't seem physically powerful enough to have caused so much damage.

But she's a witch, I reminded myself. *Maybe there was some way she could have used her magic to beat him to death. That would also explain why there wasn't any physical evidence. If she was just using the power of her mind or her magic to bash in his skull, there wouldn't have been anything to prove she'd done such a horrible thing.*

All right, I'd have to concede the possibility of magic used to commit the murder, but that still didn't explain why she would have done such a terrible thing in the first place. And if magic really had been involved, I didn't see any way how I'd ever be able to prove such a thing to the police...or the district attorney.

Much as I hated to initiate the contact, I really needed to talk to Alicia. I hadn't heard from her since seeing her on Monday at the bridal shop, although I'd gotten a pithy text from Isabella inquiring if I'd made any progress. I'd told her I was still working on it, to which she'd ominously replied that she'd see me at three o'clock on Friday afternoon, no matter what.

Luckily, my spa day in Santa Fe was scheduled for Thursday, so even if I failed miserably and had to admit defeat, at least I'd do it with nicely polished fingers and toes.

No, that wasn't going to happen. I was committed mind, body, and soul to Max Sullivan, and he was the man I'd marry on Saturday...no matter what.

Nice words. Too bad I really didn't believe them at the moment.

Max was in the family room when I got home, watching a basketball game. He wasn't as hugely into sports as he'd been in high school, but he still liked to check in on his favorite teams—in this case, the Lakers—when he had the chance. This tended to be when I wasn't around, since, unlike him, I didn't have much use for team sports of any stripe.

I paused by the sofa where he sat and said, "We need to call Alicia."

At once, he reached for the remote and turned off the TV. Luckily, he didn't seem too annoyed by the interruption, even as he asked, "Why?"

"Because I need to learn more about Lucy from her," I replied. "I need to know if there's any reason why she would have been in that awful dream."

Max got up from the couch and pulled me into his arms, then laid a soft kiss on the top of my head. "Do you really think she's going to say anything that would incriminate her daughter?"

Good question. "I don't know," I said. "All I do know is that right now, I'm just spinning my wheels. Maybe talking to her won't solve anything, but at least I'll feel as if I've done something, especially since every tick of the clock just tells me we're getting that much closer to Friday and certain doom."

He kissed me again, this time on the cheek. Those blue eyes met mine, worried but at the same time reassuring. "That 'doom' isn't certain. We're still trying to work through this. Something has to give."

Ah, Max...the eternal optimist. He always thought every problem had a solution, and never wanted to admit there were some things you just couldn't fix.

But, as he'd pointed out, we were still doing our best, and I wasn't about to throw up my hands and admit defeat.

Not yet, anyway.

"All the more reason to call Alicia," I said. "Maybe her better nature will kick in, and she'll give us some useful information."

Something about Max's expression told me he wasn't sure whether Alicia Petrucci actually had a better nature, although I knew he would never say such a thing out loud. And honestly, the way she'd treated me was awful enough that I could see why he...and I...might think that, but right now, we didn't have a lot of options.

"Okay," he said after an obvious pause. "Do you want to invite her over for dinner?"

Actually, that sounded like a great idea. We could ply her with some of Lou's amazing mushroom pizza, and hope like hell that a couple of glasses of good chianti might loosen her tongue a bit.

"Yes," I replied. "Let me call her and find out if she can make it."

TO MY RELIEF, ALICIA WAS FREE THAT night. I'd been worried that she might already have plans with her aunts or her daughter, but she said that no, Lucy had gone home to New York and didn't plan to come back until the day before the wedding.

"And she'll bring Luke with her," Alicia had added. "So you'll finally get to meet him."

I'd made what I'd hoped was an appropriately enthusiastic reply, and then we'd agreed that she'd come over at seven.

That didn't give Lou a lot of notice, but he didn't seem to mind, and only said he needed to run to the store to grab a few things and would be back as fast as possible. Al was still manning the gates and Gordon was keeping an eye on the perimeter of the property, so it wasn't as though we were being left alone. And really, with Nathan O'Rourke out of the picture, we didn't feel as dogged by the paparazzi as we had even a week earlier. True, they were still skulking around, but it seemed pretty obvious that at this point, they were just waiting for Saturday so they could grab as many wedding shots as possible. Whether their current distance had something to do with Isabella's spell—although it definitely hadn't worked at keeping Nathan O'Rourke away from me—or whether they didn't think they'd get anything useful until the big day, I didn't know. I was just glad they'd decided to back off, for whatever reason.

Max and I tidied up and set the table. The house was immaculate as always, since he had a woman named Teresa Salvatore who cleaned for him twice a week. She'd come and gone while we were in L.A. and was due back tomorrow, and would continue with her usual routine even while we were out of town on our honeymoon, guaranteeing a clean house upon our return.

If we even got to go to Italy, of course.

But at least I didn't have to worry about Alicia finding dust bunnies under the couch or less than immaculate fixtures in the powder room, and could instead focus all my energies on deciding the best way to broach the subject of her daughter's possible murderous tendencies. It wasn't the sort of thing that just naturally popped up in everyday conversation.

Wonderful smells were drifting out of the kitchen when she rang the doorbell at a few minutes past seven. I opened the door and gave her what I hoped was a natural-looking smile. "Hi, Alicia—I'm so glad you could make it over on such short notice."

"Actually, you rescued me from having dinner with my aunts...again," she responded, dark eyes twinkling a little. "So I'm very grateful for the invitation."

I raised an eyebrow. "I thought you said you didn't have plans."

"Well, nothing that wasn't eminently cancellable," she answered, her expression amused. "And of course, my aunts couldn't exactly forbid me to see my own daughter."

It crossed my mind that they'd done that very thing for years and years, just by making Alicia afraid to acknowledge my existence for fear they'd snatch me away to live in New York and marry the man they chose for me. However, I decided it was probably better not to point out that uncomfortable truth, and merely answered her smile.

"No, I suppose not," I said as I led her into the dining room. Max was already in there, uncorking a bottle of chianti.

"Hello, Max," Alicia said. "Thank you for

inviting me to your lovely home. It really is quite remarkable."

"Thank you," he replied, and reached out a hand in greeting—after setting down the corkscrew, of course. "I definitely lucked out when I found it. Would you like to sit down?"

He indicated the third chair at the table, the one directly across from the place where I usually sat. Alicia smiled and thanked him, then took a seat. I followed suit, knowing that Lou would bring the food in from the kitchen when it was ready.

Max poured wine for all of us, and raised a glass. "To family meetings," he said.

"'To family meetings,'" Alicia and I both echoed, although I privately reflected that I would have been just fine without meeting some members of my family—namely, the Petrucci elders.

Just as we were drinking our first sips of chianti, Lou came in with an enormous mushroom pizza balanced on one hand and a big bowl of green salad in the other. He somehow managed to maneuver both items to the table without spilling anything, and said, "I made this one special for you, Mrs. Petrucci."

"Alicia," she corrected him, but gently. "And it all looks amazing."

He gave a little nod, and looked almost flustered. After murmuring something about it being nothing, he fled back to the safety of the kitchen.

Hmm. Was Max's no-nonsense bodyguard a little smitten with my mother? I supposed it made some sense, since, although she looked a lot younger, they were both around the same age.

Not that I'd ever encourage such a thing. I liked Lou way too much to inflict Alicia on him.

"So," she said, after placing a slice of pizza and some salad on her plate, "I assume there was an ulterior motive for this dinner?"

Max put on one of his big-screen smiles, the kind that was so bright, you felt like you needed sunglasses to look at it directly. "Can't we entertain a family member a few days before our wedding?"

"Of course you can," she said calmly. "But considering everything else that's going on, I have to believe this isn't just about sitting down and catching up."

"Okay, you guessed it," I told her, figuring there wasn't much point in keeping up the façade any longer. "But really, our motives aren't nefarious. I only thought it might be nice to chat about Lucy and Luke, just so I don't seem totally awkward when I'm introducing them at the reception."

Maybe Alicia blinked a little. I couldn't tell for sure whether she thought there wasn't much point to such a thing when there was a very good chance the wedding wouldn't even take place, or whether she was simply wondering why all the interest now.

But then she seemed to shrug it off after taking a sip of chianti, and said, "Well, Luke is twenty-five, and Lucy is twenty-four. People sometimes called them my Irish twins, since they were born eleven months apart. They've always been very close."

Hearing that, I couldn't quite hold back a twinge of jealousy. True, my grandmother Maureen had done a wonderful job of raising me, and most of the time I'd never felt as though I lacked much, but still, I'd always wanted a brother or sister, someone I could confide in and have as an ally in what often felt like a big and uncaring world.

"You said Luke had gotten married recently?" I asked.

Alicia nodded, although her expression grew guarded. "Yes, a nice young woman named Cora."

"And your aunts chose her for him?" Max put in. His expression was one of simple curiosity and nothing more, but I knew he had to be thinking what a ridiculous custom the whole thing was in this day and age.

"Yes," she said, her tone now clipped. "But they worked very hard to find someone in our extended family who was compatible, who would make a good partner for him. She's just a year younger, and teaches at an elementary school. They get along quite well."

"Quite" well...not "very" well. I recalled how Alicia had made a brief comment about there being some friction between the two of them but decided now probably wasn't the time to bring it up, not when we were trying to act as though we were one big, happy family.

"That sounds nice," I said. "Do Luke and Cora live in Manhattan, too?"

"Yes," Alicia replied at once. She looked relieved that I'd asked such an innocuous question, and dived right in. "They have a wonderful brownstone a few blocks from my house, and the school where Cora teaches is nearby as well. I have them over for dinner at least two or three times a month, and I have to say, it's great having the whole family there."

Max reached for a second slice of pizza, having basically devoured his first piece while Alicia was talking. "Oh, Lucy still lives at home?"

"She does," Alicia said, although I noticed that faint line appear between her brows again when Max said "still." "She graduated from Columbia last year but hasn't quite decided what she wants to do with her life. Her degree is in marketing, and I suppose she'll end up with one of the big firms eventually. She just needs to decide which one."

From the way Alicia spoke, it sounded like she thought it was a foregone conclusion that her youngest child would land a prestigious job even though she was basically fresh out of college. And maybe she would. It definitely seemed as though the Petruccis were doing well for themselves, and I guessed a little subtle magic would be applied to ensure that everyone's lives went smoothly.

Well, except for Luke and Cora, who were having some difficulties. No big surprise there— even if the parties involved wanted to make things work, they still had to deal with the reality of being pushed together, of realizing they hadn't chosen each other because they'd met at a party or the library or a concert and realized there was a spark between them, were instead married because the family elders had decreed it was to be so.

"Lucy's so outgoing," I said. "I can see how marketing would be a great field for her to work in."

Alicia nodded, appearing to relax a little. "Yes, it seemed a natural choice for her."

Swirling the chianti in his glass, Max asked, "What does Luke do?"

"He works for the family trust," Alicia said. "There are quite a few assets that need to be administered."

That sounded like the kind of job someone would have been given when the family didn't know what else to do with him. Max appeared to be thinking the same thing, judging by the way one eyebrow lifted slightly.

"The Petruccis have a trust?"

Alicia sent him a very direct look, her dark eyes almost amused, as if she'd seen right though the question. "Yes, we do," she replied. "Quite a sizable one. Oh, not at the same level as the Rockefellers or the Vanderbilts, I suppose, but the Petruccis have been thriving ever since they arrived in New York a hundred years ago."

Max's mouth quirked. "I had no idea I was marrying an heiress."

"I'm not an heiress," I said quickly, even as I thought, ...*or am I?*

"Skye's case is a little complicated," Alicia said coolly. "You see, she was never formally acknowledged as a member of the family, so therefore she doesn't really have any claim to the trust. However, if she marries Christian...."

The words trailed off, and Max and I both exchanged an irritated glance.

"I'm not marrying Christian," I said, my tone flat. "I don't know how many times I have to say that to make you believe me."

Now Alicia's expression softened, and she replied, "I know you don't want to. Unfortunately, not wanting something to occur doesn't keep it from happening eventually. I know you're working very hard to discover Nathan O'Rourke's real murderer, but—"

"Oh, Skye and I are getting married on Saturday," Max cut in, but in a friendly way, as if he thought he should jump in and correct her before she embarrassed herself. "No doubt about it. We're just following up on a few things right now to be sure."

She flickered a glance toward me. "Such as?"

Should I bring up the dream?

Probably not. Although she hadn't come out and said it, I got the impression that Alicia thought the world of her darling Lucy, and would never entertain the idea that she might be a cold-blooded murderer.

Still, that didn't mean I couldn't try to come at the problem sideways.

"What else about Lucy?" I asked. "Does she have any hobbies?"

Like throwing blunt objects at people with her magic....

"She was very good at tennis in high school," Alicia said, again looking glad that we'd retreated to safer ground. "And she likes to go boating with her brother when he has the time. But she's not like you in the kitchen, Skye—you definitely inherited that talent from the O'Malley side of the family."

Something about her tone was almost condescending, as though she didn't think cooking was such a great skill to have. Well, with their kind of money, maybe the Petruccis hired cooks or went out to eat all the time. If that was the case, I thought they were definitely missing out, because as far as I was concerned, there wasn't anything better than sitting down at a table to a home-cooked meal surrounded by the people you loved.

I chose to ignore the innuendo, which could have been all in my head. When it came to dealing with Alicia Petrucci, I was always on my guard.

"Lucy's also quite the artist," Alicia added. "Not that she does much with it, but she's always sketching something. We all thought she would major in art—she surprised us by going into marketing. Then again, it's hard to say what she'll land on. Lucy's very good at surprising us."

"'Surprising' you?" Max repeated. "How so?"

"Oh, she's always been a little unpredictable," Alicia said. "She never really does what you expect her to."

"Must be hard when you need her to agree to an arranged marriage," I commented, then reached for the pizza and helped myself to another slice.

Alicia's lips thinned, and I could tell she wasn't too happy with my remark. "She has a little time," she said. "Even the elders don't expect any of us to get married before we're twenty-five. That gives people time to finish college, to learn a little bit more about ourselves. Still, I wish she wouldn't...."

The words stopped there, as if Alicia realized she'd been about to say something she really shouldn't. Max cocked an eyebrow at me, as though expecting me to jump in. I hesitated, not sure what I should say, and he seemed to guess this was the time for him to stick his oar in the water and see what happened.

"Wouldn't what?" he prompted.

Alicia took in a breath, then reached for her glass of chianti. I was sure she wasn't going to respond, was instead going to drink some wine, but then she said, "Well, I suppose we're all family here, and it would have come out sooner or later."

"What would have come out?" I asked. From her tone, it couldn't be anything good.

"Christian," she responded, then took her delayed sip of wine. "Lucy has had a crush on him for the past couple of years. Everyone's told her that he's far too old for her, but she doesn't seem to care."

I felt my eyes widen, and looked over at Max to see much the same startled expression on his face. Before I could say anything, he asked, "If she's so into Christian, then why not let her be with him? It sounds like it would solve the problem of finding someone for both of them to marry."

Alicia sent him a glare that clearly seemed intended to let him know she thought that was a ridiculous question. "Christian is twelve years older than she is," Alicia said. "That's far too big a difference. Lucy needs to find someone closer to her own age."

But my great-aunts didn't seem to have any problem hooking me up with him. Then again, most people would agree that a six-year age gap was a lot different from one that was double that number.

"How does Christian feel about all this?" I inquired. He definitely didn't seem like the type to be chasing after a twenty-four-year-old, but if the two parties involved were on board with the idea, then I didn't see the problem. They were both adults, after all.

Another swallow of wine, and Alicia said, "I think he's mostly embarrassed by her interest in him. I know he doesn't see Lucy in a romantic light at all. No, she's going to have to focus her attention elsewhere."

Her tone was firm, and I got the feeling she'd had heated discussions with her younger daughter on this topic on more than one occasion. It also seemed as though she wanted us to drop the whole thing, which was fine by me. This dinner was already awkward enough.

Somehow, I managed to guide the conversation to the reception, and the menu we had planned. My mother's expression seemed to indicate she wasn't sure the reception was going to happen at all, but at least she had enough tact not to say such a thing out loud. No, she just commented that the menu sounded wonderful, and she loved the idea of having the event in the Plaza Hotel's century-old ballroom.

And eventually, the evening was over, and she was driving her big gray BMW down the gravel lane that led to the main road. Seeing it, I thought once again of my dream and the car I'd seen as a backdrop to Nathan O'Rourke's murder. Had I only dreamed of the car because it was connected to the Petruccis, or was something else going on here?

After I'd shut the door and Max and I had reconvened in the family room, he said, "What do you make of all that?"

"You mean Lucy being obsessed with Christian?"

My fiancé nodded.

"It's a little weird," I admitted, even as I thought that was an understated way of describing the situation. "But I don't know whether it matters much. I mean, if being in love with Christian had sent Lucy into a murderous rage, you'd think I would be the victim, since her great-aunts are conspiring to get me married off to the guy and she would look at me as a roadblock to her own happiness."

"True," Max said, and rubbed his chin. Although he rarely looked tired, I could tell the strain was starting to get to him, showing in the tautness of his jaw and just the faintest shadows under his eyes. "How did she act when she met you in Santa Fe?"

"Totally nice," I replied, which was only the truth. "She seemed happy to meet me. It could have all been an act, I suppose, but I didn't get that impression. And that's even weirder, because you would think she'd see me as a rival."

Max frowned. "You're right." But then his expression immediately brightened, and he said, "But maybe she knows about the way you solve crimes and the bargain you've made with your great-aunts, and she also knows that you and I are totally in love and how you don't have any intention of marrying anyone else. Maybe she thinks that's enough to keep the elders from making a mess of everything."

That theory made some sense. At the same time, I kind of wished I had as much confidence in my abilities as Lucy Petrucci apparently did.

"Let's hope she's right," I said.

———

THAT NIGHT WHEN I LAY DOWN NEXT TO Max, I let my mind drift, but not so I could fall asleep. No, I needed to reach out to the one person I thought might be able to help me, now that pretty much all my other avenues of investigation had failed.

My grandmother Maureen.

I still didn't know exactly how I made it work, only that if I floated in this liminal state, I could find my way to that beautiful, otherworldly glade where we'd met before. And there it was, the trees fresh and green in that eternal springtime, small white flowers clustered in the grass near their trunks.

No sign of my grandmother, which didn't worry me too much. She hadn't shown up right away the other times we'd met here, either, so I knew the only thing I could do now was wait.

And yes, there she was, approaching in the same 1950s-style white dress she'd been wearing the last time I'd seen her here on this other plane, with its full skirt and Peter Pan collar. As before, she appeared looking like her younger self, hair still dark blonde and blue eyes bright.

However, those eyes now appeared very grave as she met my gaze and stopped a few paces away from where I stood. "Hello, Skye," she said.

Just hearing her voice reassured me, although I didn't see much in her expression that was terribly comforting. "I need your help, Grandma," I replied.

She nodded. "This is a terrible situation," she said. "And I really wish I could help you."

Somehow, I'd known she would answer that way, but I had no intention of letting it go without a fight. "Why not?" I demanded. "Can't you give me even a tiny little hint as to where I should be looking for Nathan O'Rourke's murderer?"

She released a breath, not quite a sigh. "It doesn't work that way. I came because I could sense your need and didn't want to leave you here without being able to speak to me, but I simply don't have any helpful information to give. The Petrucci family's magic is sort of like a shield, blurring what goes on behind it. I do think it's dreadful what they're trying to do to you and Max, and if I knew something, of course I would tell you."

My heart fell as if it was going to sink right down to my toes. If the spirit of my grandmother couldn't even help me, how in the world was I supposed to figure this all out on my own?

Before I could offer another protest, though, she came to me and laid a gentle hand against my cheek. Her fingers were warm, and felt utterly human. It definitely wasn't the touch of a woman who'd died more than three years earlier.

"I have faith in you, sweetheart," she told me. "You'll figure this out, if only because you and Max are meant to be together, and true love always wins in the end. Remember that."

Another butterfly touch against my cheek, and then she was gone, fading away as I watched. I put my own hand up to my face, to feel the place where she'd caressed me and offered what reassurance she could.

True love always wins in the end.

I'd have to hold that belief close, no matter what else might happen during the next few days.

CHAPTER 14

Polishing It Off

I woke up the next morning with a knot in my stomach that had nothing to do with the wonderful pizza I'd consumed the night before. No, this was all about Isabella Petrucci's looming deadline and the miserable realization that I didn't have any more clue as to who had killed Nathan Petrucci than I had the day before...not to mention the knowledge that I'd tried to play my last card with my grandmother, only to have it all come to nothing.

Despite my worries and the awful way the clock kept ticking down to my doom, I knew I had to get out of bed and pretend everything was fine. Luckily, I'd talked Deanne and Darcy down from a bachelorette party—their first idea had been to take me to Albuquerque for some kind of male strip show—and instead all we were doing was going to

Santa Fe for the day, to a spa at La Fonda that promised a day of pampering. Still, I was going to have to act normal around my two friends, which I knew would be a lot easier said than done.

But we weren't meeting until eleven...the plan was to have lunch first and then go to the spa...so that meant I had some time to try to steady myself.

"It's going to be okay," Max told me after we'd poured our morning coffee and wandered out to the patio so we could drink it at the table there and enjoy the view. Yes, it was still chilly in the morning even though we'd been getting those astonishing seventy-degree days one after the other, but we were both wearing sweatshirts over our usual morning attire—pajama bottoms and a T-shirt for him, leggings and a long tank for me.

"You're going to keep saying that even after Christian Petrucci slips a ring on my finger," I snapped, and Max sent me a piercing look, the kind he usually reserved for the film roles where he had to defuse a bomb or interrogate a terrorist.

"Would you rather I threw my hands up in the air and said 'oh, well'?"

Instantly contrite, I reached over to lay a hand on his. "I'm sorry," I said. "It's just that I've been going out of my mind trying to figure out who would have really had a motive for killing Nathan, and I keep coming up with nothing. The only thing I can think of is that Lucy might have killed him because he got in Christian's face, but that doesn't even make sense. If anything, you'd think she would be proud of what Christian had done, and would have looked at Nathan as the guy who'd made Christian appear that much more desirable."

Max wrapped his fingers around mine, his skin warm, while mine was slightly chilled by the brisk morning air. "Do you think slugging a guy makes a man more desirable?"

"No," I replied. "I mean, I'm not a huge fan of violence. But we're not talking about me. We're talking about Lucy and her fixation on Christian."

A moment passed while Max stared out into the golden hillsides that surrounded the ranch, just the slightest bit blurred by morning haze. "I think it's time to go to your great-aunts with this."

That was the absolute last thing I wanted to do. All I had to go on was a single dream, and one that had felt hazy and off-kilter at best. Yes, it had seemed true despite all that, but I had a feeling the Petrucci witches might not see things the same way.

But, considering it was the only real piece of evidence I had left, I knew it would be foolish not to act upon it. They might be dismissive...actually, I knew they would be...and yet I didn't have many options.

"All right," I said wearily. "But let's make some omelets first. I know I'm going to need my strength up for this."

My three great-aunts stared at me as if I'd suddenly suggested we should go for a camel ride in Zanzibar.

"You think *Lucy* killed Nathan O'Rourke?" Isabella demanded at last.

Carmela chimed in, "Lucy is a sweet girl. She's simply not capable of doing anything like that."

And Vittoria added, "Dreams are very unreliable things, you know."

I glared at her, since she was the last one who'd spoken. "Regular dreams, sure," I replied. "I'm not talking about those kinds of dreams. I'm talking about true dreams, the ones I've been having since I was little. Sometimes they're hard to interpret, but they're almost always right."

"*Almost* is not the same as *always*," Isabella intoned.

Of course she would seize on that part of my remark. "Close enough," I said. "Dreams and tea leaves have always guided me in the right direction."

Carmela sniffed. "Chancy magic, not anything you can depend on."

Was that a sideways slam at my O'Malley magic?

"It's been more dependable than your Petrucci stuff," I shot back.

"Because you haven't been trained properly," Vittoria broke in. "Alicia made a very great mistake in showing you just a little and then leaving you to your own devices."

"Well, I guess you need to talk to Alicia about that—" I began, and Isabella held up a hand.

"Enough of all this. Arguing isn't going to get us anywhere." Her two sisters fell into a sulky silence, although I guessed from the death glares they were shooting in my direction that they considered the topic far from settled. After waiting a beat or two, Isabella went on, "I appreciate you coming to us with your concerns, Skye, but we've known Lucy since the day she was born. She simply isn't capable of the kind of violence that took Nathan O'Rourke's life—and I'm fairly certain you know that deep down as well, even if you don't want to admit it to yourself."

Since Max and I had thought about the same thing, there wasn't much point in arguing with my great-aunt. Still....

"Have you talked to Lucy?" I asked. "Do any of you even know what she was doing last Friday night?"

Vittoria sent me a glance of venomous triumph. "As a matter of fact, we do. She was at home in New York—I spoke to her that evening, and she told me she had just gotten back from having dinner with some friends."

An alibi that could be easily corroborated, I supposed...except for the teensy little detail about Nathan's time of death being pegged around 2 or 3 a.m. local time, which would have been somewhere between four and five o'clock in the morning in New York. That meant Lucy could have had her dinner with friends and then popped over here in the dead of night when she didn't think she had any chance of being detected.

That was the problem when dealing with someone who could teleport so easily...she could come and go with no one even noticing, could be back in the home she shared with Alicia in New York without giving any indication that she'd done anything other than sleep peacefully in her bed.

I opened my mouth to say as much...then slowly closed it again. It was painfully obvious to me that the Petrucci elders weren't going to budge on this one, that they believed Lucy was above reproach and couldn't possibly have taken that baseball bat—or whatever it was—to Nathan O'Rourke's skull.

"All right," I said, "let's begin with believing in Lucy's innocence. If that's the case, then why would I have seen her in my dream?"

Carmela placed her hands on her hips, her expression bordering on smug. "That's easy enough. You're jealous of your half-sister, so your subconscious made her the villain in your dream."

Was I jealous of Lucy? Did some part of me wish I'd gotten even half the love and attention Alicia had obviously showered on her younger daughter?

As soon as those questions popped up in my mind, I dismissed them as self-doubt and nothing more. To be perfectly honest, I didn't like Alicia all that much, and even though it had taken me a lot of years to get over being abandoned by her the way I had, I now realized I wouldn't have changed anything about my life. It had been much better for me to be raised here in Las Vegas by my loving grandmother, rather than in the stifling embrace of the Petrucci family.

"It's not jealousy," I returned. "This is the universe trying to tell me something."

At those words, Carmela sniffed. "Ridiculous O'Malley magic—signs and portents, dreams and tea leaves. They're nothing you can rely on."

My eyes narrowed, and right then I wished I had better control of the Petrucci magic, just so I could use it to infest my great-aunt's armpits with a million fleas or something else extremely uncomfortable but not life-threatening. However, since I certainly didn't have the skills to pull off such a stunt, I had to settle for sending her an evil glare.

"They've done enough for me so far," I said. "I wouldn't have been able to solve any of those other murders if it hadn't been for my dreams and tea leaves. And they're definitely trying to tell me something now. I just haven't been able to figure out what that is."

"Better hurry," Vittoria said in poisonously sweet tones. "Because time is running out."

Clearly, this had been a terrible idea. I straightened, and tugged at the hem of the pretty embroidered blouse I'd put on in anticipation of my trip to Santa Fe with Deanne and Darcy. "Fine—don't believe me. But I'm still going to keep working on this."

Throughout the previous exchanges, Isabella had been silent, apparently content to let me spar with her sisters. Now, though, she only said coolly, "You go ahead with that, Skye. But we will see you here tomorrow afternoon."

Oh, they were all impossible. Without bothering to reply, I hitched my purse up on my shoulder and headed for the door. As much as I wanted to slam it, though, I knew such a show of anger wouldn't do me any good—and would only annoy the innocent people who'd had the bad luck to book hotel rooms on the same floor as my great-aunts.

Instead, I left the door standing open and stalked over to the stairs, then made my way to the ground floor of the hotel. As I went, I reflected that it was going to take a lot of back massages to release even a tenth of the pent-up tension I was holding in my body.

———

WHAT HELPED A LOT WERE THE MARGARITAS that Deanne and Darcy and I had with our lunch at the La Fonda Hotel. The two prickly pear drinks I downed started to smooth out the rough edges, and by the time we were done with our Shiatsu massages and hot rock treatments and facials and mani/pedis, I was starting to feel almost like a human being again.

"I could get used to this," Darcy said as we rolled out of the spa later that afternoon, all glowing and fresh and looking like new women. She sent me a sly sideways glance. "I don't suppose Max has any unattached co-stars who might be interested in a torrid affair with a cute deputy from a small town?"

I couldn't help grinning. "Not that I'm aware of, but I'll let you know."

The spa day had been my treat, obviously—neither Deanne nor Darcy had the kind of spare funds to spend on those kinds of luxuries. Normally, I wouldn't either, but since Max had added me to his Centurion Amex account, I had access to funds I would never have even dreamed of a couple of years earlier.

"And everything's set for the rehearsal dinner tomorrow night," Deanne put in. "I got a text from Skyler that they've put the signs up in the windows and posted on their social media to let everyone know they're going to be closed for a special event."

Renting out Smoky Joe's for the dinner had been Deanne's idea, and I had to admit it was a good one. There weren't a lot of places in Las Vegas that had the room for that kind of gathering, and since the owners of the restaurant continued to feel like they owed Max a favor for giving them the funds they needed to finish their remodel after the *Fix My Town* people bailed, they obviously hadn't thought twice about letting us rent the space on what would have been one of their busiest nights of the week.

"Good," I said. "Then it sounds as if we're ready to go. Andie and I finalized everything at the hotel, so now we mostly just have to wait."

And pray that I can figure out who really killed Nathan O'Rourke before then, I thought. *Or that rehearsal dinner ain't happening.*

Obviously, I couldn't say anything about that to either of my bridesmaids, both of whom probably shrugged off any nervousness on my part as pre-wedding jitters. No, we just chatted about the flowers and the food, and the hotel rooms Max had booked so we'd have someplace to change before the ceremony. The two of us had already decided to go back to the house after the reception rather than stay at the hotel, partly because we couldn't think of anywhere we'd rather be on our wedding night than the ranch that would be our home, and partly because it was just easier to leave for the airport from there.

The closer we got to Las Vegas on our return trip, though, the tenser I felt, all the hard work of the spa's excellent masseuses almost completely erased as my neck and shoulders kept tightening up. While I was away getting pampered, it had been easy to forget tomorrow's looming deadline, but now the reality of it all was hitting me in the face.

Twenty-four hours from now, I'd have to confront my aunts. And if I couldn't produce the actual murderer and get the charges against Christian dropped, my carefully curated future would fall to pieces.

Deanne dropped me off at the ranch, told me she'd see me the following night at Smoky Joe's, and then headed back into town so she could take Darcy home. While I actually didn't have much else to do—it had been the simple truth that the wedding was mostly a waiting game at this point— I knew she still had a lot of work to handle on Friday, like double-checking everything with the florist and the officiant and the photographer, and making sure the band remembered that they had to be on-site and ready to go no later than seven o'clock that Saturday night. The ceremony itself was scheduled for five, and Max and I had already planned to use the time while the room was being reconstituted as a reception space to take our photographs in various places around the hotel.

It all sounded as though it would go perfectly. The main problem was that I still didn't know if it would happen at all.

Lou was making chicken piccata in the kitchen —I'd told him I needed to eat light these last couple of days, just to be safe—and Max, as I'd thought, had planted himself in the family room so he could continue watching the playoffs.

"How're the Lakers doing?" I asked as I bent to give him a kiss.

"Crappy," he said with a grin. "You smell incredible."

"Thanks," I replied. Some pretty amazing lotions had been rubbed into my skin while I was at the spa, and I assumed that was what Max had noticed. "It was a nice day, but...."

"I know," he said, and reached up to take my hand so he could guide me down to a seat on the couch next to him. "I don't suppose any of those massages helped spark some inspiration?"

"No," I replied, knowing how dejected I sounded. "Max, what are we supposed to do?"

"Well," he said, "if we really can't come up with

any solid leads before tomorrow afternoon, I think the only thing we can do is throw ourselves on your aunts' mercy and try to appeal to their better natures."

Fat chance.

"I don't think they have any," I responded, and released a breath. "But since I don't have any better ideas, I suppose it's worth a try."

We sat there in silence for a moment, both of us trying to draw strength and reassurance from the other person's presence. But even though I usually found Max infinitely comforting, I couldn't help worrying if this was going to be one of the last times I was able to do this, whether after tomorrow, I'd have to learn some way to find happiness with Christian Petrucci...assuming he wasn't locked up in prison for life.

My heart and soul didn't want to accept any of that, even as my brain tried to point out that we really didn't have many options left to us. Running away wouldn't work, not when the Petrucci elders appeared to possess the ability to find us no matter where we went. No, we'd have to face this head on and do our best.

Even if that best felt like anything but right now.

CHAPTER 15

Seventh-Inning Stretch

That night I had a hard time falling asleep. Max and I had made love, urgently, passionately, as if we both somehow knew this was a chance that might not come again. And after we were done and I heard his breathing deepen into the steady rhythms of sleep, I lay there in the darkness, eyes wide as I stared at the ceiling.

What was I missing? Why had I dreamed of Lucy when it seemed clear to everyone involved that she couldn't possibly have killed Nathan O'Rourke?

I had no idea, just as I had no idea what those two wavy lines in my tea-leaf reading were supposed to represent. Right now, all those clues felt completely random, unconnected to one another, and I just didn't know what I should do next.

Actually, what I really wanted to do was break down and have a good cry...not because it would do any good, but simply because it might help to loosen the tense little knot that seemed to have wedged itself permanently in my solar plexus.

But I didn't want to wake up Max...and I also didn't want to give my great-aunts the satisfaction of seeing me with red, puffy eyes when I went to meet them tomorrow afternoon. No, I was going to walk into this with my head held high, no matter what.

Damn them, though. Damn them all.

Maybe that was better. Maybe if I was angry, filled with righteous rage, then I wouldn't have time to be sad. None of this was my fault, after all. I wasn't a real detective—I was just a woman with a couple of peculiar abilities that had come in useful now and again. Expecting me to find out who the true guilty party was in all of this was ridiculous.

I lay there, and brooded into the darkness...and eventually let it claim me.

BECAUSE LOU WAS MAKING US BREAKFAST the next morning, Max and I couldn't exactly talk about the massive problem looming over us, and had to pretend we were happy and looking forward to our big day tomorrow.

"I knew," he said as he slipped a perfect roasted pepper and onion frittata onto my plate. "I knew as soon as you came over here that you were the girl for Max."

"Oh, really?" I replied, while across the table, Max did his best to smother a grin.

"Sure," Lou said. "Not that I'd been working for him long back then, but I could tell he was happy to be back in New Mexico, and it just made sense he should have a nice New Mexico girl in his life rather than one of those Hollywood types."

Max picked up his mug of coffee and sipped from it, then observed, "Very true. Not that I was really thinking along those lines when I signed on for the role that brought me back here, but when I saw Skye that first time after all those years, I knew I'd come back where I was meant to be."

I couldn't help blushing a little at those words. Not for the first time, I wished we hadn't been dancing around each other all those months, that we'd been more open with one another. We could have had so much time together...time that now felt even more precious, since there was a very real chance we wouldn't get any more.

"It does feel fated," I said lightly, since I couldn't really say anything else. Both Lou and Al were still in the dark about what might be happening a few short hours from now, and I needed to keep it that way. We couldn't exactly tell them the truth about the Petruccis, partly because I doubted those two gruff, no-nonsense men would even allow themselves to that believe that witches existed, and partly because they might take it into their minds to intervene. I couldn't risk that. Bad enough that my horrible family was about to break Max's heart, but I couldn't allow Al and Lou to get hurt as well...or Gordon, although he'd never grown close to us the way the two other body-guards had. He looked on this as a job and nothing else, while Lou and Al felt like part of the family.

Lou seemed to understand that Max and I wanted this time to ourselves, because he told us to enjoy our breakfasts and headed back into the kitchen.

Although the food in front of me looked deli-cious—there was a little bowl of sliced fruit in addi-tion to the frittata—I wasn't sure whether I'd be able to force any of it down.

"You need to eat," Max said quietly, and I looked up from my plate to see him gazing at me, blue eyes deadly serious. "I know you're worried, but whatever happens today, better to do it with enough fuel in your system."

Despite everything, I couldn't help smiling. "You sound like my grandmother."

"Well, Maureen was a wise woman," he replied. "She would definitely tell you that you can't think straight on an empty stomach."

"And that breakfast is the most important meal of the day," I added, still smiling as I remembered the way she would encourage me to eat some oatmeal or at least a piece of toast and an apple when I was ready to tear out the door. Back in those days, I often ran late in the morning, always fussing with my hair or my outfit, trying to come up with the perfect look that might prevent me from getting teased by the mean girls. None of those strategies ever really worked, although I usually tried to follow my grandmother's advice and eat something before I headed out to face the big, bad world.

Max nodded. "Exactly."

Feeling a little more energized, I picked up my fork and ate a few bites of frittata, then followed them with some pieces of strawberry and a couple of blueberries. While the food didn't bestow upon me the power to successfully conquer my great-aunts, it did taste good, and I had to hope it would spark something in my brain that would help me solve my dilemma.

Taking a cue from me, Max ate some of his breakfast as well, and we proceeded in silence for a couple of minutes, as if neither one of us wanted to interrupt the quiet with conversation that would only drive home how precarious our situation really was.

After I'd finished most of my frittata, I said,

"Well, that was good, but it didn't provide any sparks of inspiration."

"Same here," Max replied as he pushed his now-empty plate aside. He reached for his cup of coffee and drained the remaining liquid in the mug, then set it down next to his plate. "So...what next? Do you think you should try looking at some tea leaves again?"

"Because that helped me so much last time," I said sourly. There was still some more coffee in my mug, but I realized I'd had enough, that, despite the food in my system, I still felt jangly and worried, every nerve ending shrilling as though to tell me I only had six hours before I had to go and confront my aunts in their rooms at the Plaza Hotel.

Although he didn't reach out to squeeze my hand, his gaze was somehow comforting anyway, his blue eyes an echo of the skies beyond the dining room window. "Sometimes you need to try a couple of times," he reminded me. "It's not time to give up yet."

No, that would be six hours from now.

On the other hand, lacking any other clues, it seemed as if I might as well take another whack at the tea leaves. The worst thing that might happen would be that I wasted some time, and since I didn't have anything else to do at the moment, I might as well give it a shot.

"All right," I said, then stood and gathered up our empty plates. "You can shower while I'm working on it."

"Sounds like a plan."

He got up as well, and gave me a soft, gentle kiss before heading out of the dining room and down the hall to the main suite. I took the plates into the kitchen, glad to see that Lou had apparently decamped. No, it wasn't that I minded having him around, but it was always easier to get a decent reading when I could be assured of my solitude.

The water in the kettle was still warm, so it didn't take too long to get it back to near boiling. Soon enough, I'd poured the hot water over the tea leaves, and taken the cup and its accompanying saucer back into the dining room. Usually, I did this sort of thing in my office, but I was hoping that a change of venue might break loose some of the cobwebs that seemed to be crowding my brain.

All right, everything was set up. Now I just had to decide what I wanted to ask. I hadn't gotten far last time trying to query who the murderer was, so maybe I needed to go about this in a different way.

How is Lucy Petrucci connected to Nathan O'Rourke's death?

I held the thought in my mind as I drank the tea, and continued to keep it floating in my thoughts as I dribbled out the last of the liquid with the teacup upside down on its saucer. Then it was time to turn it right-side up and take a look at the cup's interior.

Same blob at the bottom, same two odd little lines on roughly the equator of the teacup.

Why those two lines? I'd already established that a fence didn't make any sense in the situation, but what else could they be? An equal sign turned on its side?

That answer didn't make any more sense than my fence theory did.

I resisted the urge to fling the teacup against the wall. Doing so wouldn't have fixed the situation, and also, the cup had belonged to my great-grandmother, was one of the precious items she'd brought with her to America from Ireland. I could never hurt something that was one of the few heirlooms she'd managed to pass down to her descendants.

Still, the leaves were trying to tell me something, or they wouldn't have shown me the same symbol twice in a row. It wasn't their fault that I was too dense to figure it out.

I got up from my chair and went back into the kitchen, then rinsed out the teacup and cleaned the saucer before drying them with a tea towel and putting them back in their place of honor in one of the cupboards.

A couple of lines.

What did they mean?

I didn't know...and if the answer didn't present itself in the very near future, both Max and I were in a lot of trouble.

WE BOTH TRIED TO ACT AS NORMAL AS WE could, but that was easier said than done. Max's mom called a little after one and even asked if he was doing okay because he sounded so strange. He assured her that everything was fine and that we were both just a little tense because of all the things that needed to be done in the next twenty-four hours, and luckily, his explanation appeared to be assurance enough. When he set down the phone, though, his expression was strained.

"This is harder than I'd thought it would be," he said. "I thought I could push everything to the back of my mind, but...."

"I know," I replied. "It's awful. Maybe we should have gone to the movies or something."

Because Las Vegas's one and only movie theater had gotten fixed up the same time as Smoky Joe's and for much the same reason—they were both projects started by the *Fix My Town* team and then completed thanks to Max's financial contributions after the production company bailed—going there was now a lot more fun than it used to be, with real reclining seats and some gourmet options at the concession stand.

"Being someplace that public probably wouldn't have been a very good idea," he said, and I was forced to reluctantly agree. "I know the paparazzi haven't been as over the top now that Nathan O'Rourke is out of the picture, but I'm sure they must be on the prowl today, considering the wedding's tomorrow."

True. Walking down Bridge Street like we were a couple of regular people probably wasn't something we should be doing right now. Just going to the Plaza Hotel had its own issues, but because we could park behind Levitation Latte and walk most of the way in the alley, it was a little easier than strolling down the main drag like we didn't have a care in the world.

"Then we can watch some TV here," I said. "Because I need something to occupy my mind, or otherwise I'm going to go crazy."

And that's what we ended up doing—snuggling up next to each other on the sofa in the family room, breathing in each other's company. We watched a couple of old episodes of *Longmire*, mostly because it was just fun to see our hometown in so many of the background shots. Many of those scenes included the sheriff's office, which was really just a door between an antique store and the gallery where Max had bought the painting that now hung in a place of pride in the living room.

I couldn't help reflecting, though, that I would have happily traded places with Absaroka County's sheriff. At least he always seemed able to solve the crimes that crossed his path, even if he sometimes got bloodied along the way.

Then it was a quarter until three, and we could no longer ignore the horrible deadline that loomed only fifteen minutes away.

"I guess we'd better get going," Max said, and I reluctantly got up from the couch and went to retrieve my purse, which I'd left sitting on a side table.

"Maybe we should still make a break for it," I said as we headed toward the door. "My great-aunts can't possibly know everything."

"I doubt they do," Max replied. His manner was subdued but also resolute, as if he knew there was nothing we could do to avoid what was about to come next. "But they probably know enough. Since we don't have a clear idea of what they can and can't do, it's hard to say whether they set some kind of surveillance spell on the ranch to be able to tell exactly when we're coming and going."

That sounded exactly like something the Petrucci elders would do.

"You have a point," I replied.

Max reached out and took my hand. "Let's go."

I didn't say anything, only followed him out to the garage and got into the Bronco. Someone viewing me from the outside might have said I appeared preternaturally calm. Inside, though, I was raging—at my aunts, at the universe for not providing the clues I needed...hell, at Nathan O'Rourke himself, who'd gotten into Christian's face for no good reason.

Okay, victim-blaming was never a good look, but I couldn't help myself right then, not when I was about to lose the only man I'd ever truly wanted.

Max seemed calm himself...unless you looked closer at his hands and saw the way his knuckles stood out as he wrapped his fingers around the steering wheel. I wished there was something I could say to him to make this all better, but of course there wasn't.

Nothing could make this better, except the murderer suddenly deciding to turn him—or her—self in.

We'd already agreed to park behind Levitation Latte, so Max pulled into one of the spaces there, and did his usual pause to check our surroundings and make sure no paparazzi were lurking nearby. The coast was clear, though, which made sense. My shop was closed for the next few weeks, and there would be no reason for any of those photographers to believe I'd be anywhere nearby.

That was why we were able to walk down the alleyway unmolested, and to hurry the last few steps to the front door of the Plaza Hotel without anyone taking any particular notice of us. Because we already knew which rooms my great-aunts were currently occupying, we didn't bother to stop at the front desk but continued to the stairs and headed up to the second floor.

Isabella answered my knock immediately, my hand still halfway in the air when she answered the door. Her expression one of fierce triumph, she let us in.

"I assume you haven't discovered who the murderer is," she said.

"No," I replied, after exchanging a quick glance with Max. He gave me a very brief nod, as though letting me know it was okay for me to do the talking. "We're still working on the evidence."

"Then you're done," Carmela put in. "The terms of our agreement were that you must marry Christian if you didn't locate the real killer before three o'clock today."

That knot in my stomach seemed to tighten even further, and for a queasy second or two, I didn't know whether or not I was going to be sick.

Maybe I could get my aunts to reconsider if I barfed all over their shoes.

Then I blurted, "Those were the terms of *your* agreement. I need more time!"

Max stepped in there, saying, "What's the difference if you stop the wedding now or tomorrow at the same time? The ceremony isn't supposed to start until five, but those extra twenty-four hours or so could make all the difference."

Isabella looked over at Carmela and Vittoria, both of whom shook their heads.

No surprise.

However, my great-aunt startled me by asking, "Do you really think an extra day will make any difference?"

"It might," Max replied. "Look at it this way—the longer we play along with you, the longer people will think everything is fine. We can have our rehearsal dinner tonight with no one the wiser, and Skye and I can keep digging. If we still don't come up with anything by tomorrow afternoon, then fine. We'll surrender. You can even interrupt the ceremony by raising an objection and being all theatrical about it, if that's what floats your boat. But maybe we'll have found a clue by then."

Isabella went silent again, and I hardly dared to breathe. Could she really be considering whether or not to give us a break?

"Very well," she said at last, and I wanted to slump with relief. However, I managed to continue standing next to Max, chin up, as she went on, "But no more than a day. I honestly don't think it will make any difference, but if you want to continue to cling to false hope for that much longer, so be it."

"Isabella—" Carmela began, clearly about to launch into a series of protests, but her older sister just shook her head.

"This changes nothing," Isabella said, her tone firm enough that Carmela shut her mouth. "These two haven't found anything useful so far, and there's no reason to believe they'll do any better over the course of the next twenty-four hours... especially when they have so much they need to do in order to get ready for their wedding and keep up the façade that everything is all right."

Max's lips compressed at those words, and I could tell he wasn't too thrilled with Isabella's vote of no confidence. But since we'd gained an extra day, he obviously wasn't going to argue with her.

"Thank you," I said, and put my hand in Max's, tugging a little so he'd know this was our time to exit stage left. "We'll see you tomorrow."

"At four," Isabella intoned...as if we could have forgotten.

A little giddy with relief—even though I knew this was a temporary reprieve and nothing more, despite her giving us an extra hour—I replied, "Not a problem. I'll just have to figure out a way to extricate myself from my bridesmaids, since we'll be here at the hotel and getting ready by then."

"Whatever it takes," Isabella told me, then added ominously, "If you're not here at four, then we'll come in search of you."

Since there wasn't any easy way to respond to her veiled threat, I only ducked my head and continued to back toward the door.

"Thanks!" Max called out, just as we slipped into the hallway.

No time to pause for a sigh of relief. Instead, we hurried toward the stairs and outside, and took deep gulps of air once we knew we were safely away.

"Did we really just get Isabella to agree to another day?" Max said as we strode toward the alley and his Bronco where it waited for us behind my coffee shop.

"Sure looks like it," I replied, and flashed him a relieved smile. "Now we just have to figure out what to do with that time."

NOT MUCH THAT CONTRIBUTED TO solving the case, unfortunately. By the time we got back to the ranch, it was almost four o'clock, and we knew we had to return downtown in only a couple of hours for the rehearsal dinner. As much as I would have liked to cancel the whole thing—was it really necessary to devote that much time to walking down an imaginary aisle?—I knew it was way too late in the game to call it off.

Instead, Max and I went into his office and

closed the door so we could brainstorm. This wasn't ordinary behavior for us, since we really didn't mind either Al or Lou overhearing whatever we might have to say, but in this case, we didn't have much choice. Normally, one of the body-guards would be on duty and the other either at home or running errands or—in Lou's case—making meals from time to time. Right now, though, with the wedding so close, both of them were physically at the ranch as much as they could be, just in case any intrepid paparazzi tried to snap some photos of the happy couple on the day before their wedding.

"All right," Max said, "let's try to do this the way a cop would." He was holding a clipboard and trying to look official, a plan that was foiled slightly by the Ski Santa Fe T-shirt and faded jeans he was currently wearing. I'd almost asked him to change for our meeting with the great-aunts but had decided to let it go.

After all, they hadn't shown either one of us very much respect, so I didn't see why we should return the favor.

"And how is that?" I asked, trying not to smile. Yes, the situation was serious, but I had to believe that the mere fact of us being together right now when a few hours earlier we'd thought we'd hit the end of the road meant the universe was doing its best to ensure we got the happy ending we'd been hoping for.

"Well, by being methodical, for one thing," Max replied. "That's why I think it's a good idea for us to write down absolutely everything we know about the case. Sometimes getting stuff down in one place is enough to spark an idea."

I couldn't argue with that suggestion, not when we'd been a little scattered with our fact-finding. True, we'd been doing all this while also having to get ready for our wedding, so I supposed we could be excused for not being quite as laser-focused as we should be.

"All right," I said. "Let's go."

We spent the next hour or so writing down every single detail we could recall—Jana Donalds' affair with Nathan, the gray car from my dream, the recurring pair of wavy lines that the teacups kept wanting to show me, even Nathan's litigious neighbor Todd, who admittedly didn't seem to have much to do with any of it.

At the end, though, I just let out a sigh and shook my head.

"There's nothing new here," I complained. "We've gone over all of this multiple times. The problem is there's a big gaping hole in all these facts where our murderer should be."

Max ran a hand through his sun-streaked hair, mussing locks that had already been rumpled the same way numerous times during our convo. "I know," he said, sounding dejected. "I kept hoping if we put all our information together, we might come up with something, but right now, I'm not seeing any patterns that make sense."

That's because there aren't any, I thought, but I kept the observation to myself. We were both already discouraged enough, and I didn't see the point in making matters worse.

"Well, maybe it'll come to us after we sleep on it," I told him. "In the meantime, we need to get ready for the rehearsal dinner and head over to Smoky Joe's."

Max made a face, although he didn't bother to contradict me. He knew as well as I did that we needed to make an appearance tonight and act as though everything was okay...even while things were about as far from okay as they could possibly be.

As far as I could tell, no one at the rehearsal dinner seemed to notice anything off about either Max or me. We were a group of about twenty altogether—Max's parents, the members of the wedding party...Deanne and Darcy and me, and then Max and Deanne's husband Mike and an actor named Ellis Fields, who had been roommates with Max when he first moved to L.A. and with whom he'd remained close. Ellis was successful in his own right, if not quite at Max's level, and extremely good-looking. I knew Darcy was more than happy to be paired up with him for the ceremony, and was probably hoping to spend as much of the reception in his company as she could.

Otherwise, there was the officiant, the pastor from Deanne's church. He was a quiet man in his late forties who had promised to give us a nice, friendly ceremony that wasn't overly church-y, since neither Max nor I was particularly religious. My relatives from Texas, who rarely visited, had come to Las Vegas for the ceremony, and had brought with them my little cousin Emma, the flower girl, and her brother Ollie, the ring-bearer, which was why all of them needed to be here for the rehearsal dinner.

All in all, it was a cordial enough group, although I couldn't help being relieved when the evening was over and Max and I could escape back to the ranch.

"Now we just have to get through tomorrow," he said as he pulled the Bronco into the garage.

I managed a wavery smile. "Easier said than done. Unless I have a dream tonight that points to the murderer with a big flaming red arrow, I don't know how we're going to make this work."

He reached over and placed a reassuring hand

on my leg. I'd put on a blue silk cocktail dress for the dinner—the kind of gown I would never have worn before I was with Max—and I could feel the heat of his fingers right through the thin fabric.

"Well, maybe you will," he said, the warmth of his smile obvious in the glow from the Bronco's instrument panel. "Never say die, that's my motto."

One that fit Max to a T, although I didn't think I could be nearly that confident.

But shooting him down right now would only be cruel, so I just nodded. "It's true," I said. "So let's both send out a prayer to the universe that this will all become clear to us before morning."

He gave my leg a little squeeze, then let go. "Damn straight. And maybe we can have a little nightcap to give us some courage."

Normally, I didn't drink anything beyond whatever I might have had with dinner, but tonight the idea of a little something extra sounded good to me. Just a small glass of that late-harvest malbec we'd bought at a wine shop in Santa Fe a while back, and maybe that would be enough to help me relax into sleep...and, with any luck, open the doorway to a true dream, one that would help me understand what the first one had been trying to tell me.

We went inside the house. Al was on duty at the gate and Lou was walking the perimeter, although Gordon had gone home for the night. Prowling the borders of the property definitely didn't sound like much fun...especially since the two bodyguards were going to be our faithful shadows the next day as well...but they'd both insisted.

"Both of us have gone without sleep plenty of times," Al told us, and Lou nodded.

"Besides, we'll have lots of time to catch up on our sleep when you're on your honeymoon," he added, and that seemed to be the end of it.

At any rate, we had the place to ourselves this evening, and I knew exactly what I wanted to do with that solitude. One quiet drink, and then we could slip away to the bedroom and forget our troubles in each other's arms. We'd been granted this reprieve, and I wanted to make the best of it.

Max poured us some of the late-harvest wine into small hand-blown glasses that I thought had been originally intended for tequila but worked well for this purpose, too. Armed with our after-dinner wine, we headed into the living room.

No toast either of us could offer and have it seem genuine. Instead, we clinked our glasses together and raised them to take a sip...

...only to be interrupted by Lucy Petrucci materializing in the middle of the living room, her slender body practically quivering with indignation.

"How *could* you!" she cried.

CHAPTER 16

Gemini Divide

For a second or two, I could only stare at my half-sister in shock. Then I managed to find my voice and said, "How could I what?"

Next to me, Max was blinking. Even though he'd seen the great-aunts pull this same disappearing and reappearing act, it looked as though he was having a hard time adjusting to the way Lucy had just popped into the middle of our living room out of nowhere.

She took a step forward, dark eyes blazing with fury. "How could you go to our great-aunts and tell them that you suspected me of murder?"

Oh, boy. I glanced over at Max, who only gave a very small nod, as though telling me he'd handle this.

Probably a good idea. I already felt as though I was walking on eggshells with Lucy, wondering if my fiancé's comment about her being jealous could actually have some merit. I didn't want to believe such a thing was possible, but right now, I was more than happy to have Max step in as my defender.

"Skye had a dream—" he began.

He didn't get any farther than that, however, because Lucy planted her hands on her hips, dark eyes—so like mine—practically shooting laser beams.

I supposed I should be glad that was one talent I didn't think she possessed.

"A *dream?*" she said, cutting him off before he could go any further. "Dreams don't mean anything! That's why they're dreams!"

I'd never been any good at confrontations, but Max appeared to take that volley of exclamation points in stride.

"In most cases, sure," he said easily. Hands in the pockets of his dress pants—neither one of us had taken the time to change out of our "good" clothes—he rocked back on the heels of his shiny wingtips, looking as if he didn't have a care in the world. "But Skye has true dreams, ones that sometimes show her the past and the future. They've helped us more than once when we were trying to solve a murder. So, it shouldn't seem too strange that she'd want to take her suspicions to your great-aunts."

None of these logical arguments appeared to have made much of an impact, judging by the way Lucy's eyes narrowed further. Not bothering to respond directly to Max, she looked over at me, red angry spots showing on her cheeks.

"Can't you stick up for yourself? Do you need someone else to do everything for you?"

I told myself to count to three...better yet, ten... and made sure I took in a deep breath before I allowed myself to reply. "Max is doing a good enough job that I didn't think I needed to step in," I said calmly. "But sure, I can stick up for myself... when it's worth my time. I went to the elders because I didn't feel as if the dream was something I should keep to myself. That's all. It wasn't like some dedicated campaign against you or anything."

"Right," she said, still staring daggers at me. "I know you just wanted to make me look bad so you could have Christian all to yourself."

Oh, for God's sake....

"If I really wanted Christian," I said tartly, "then I wouldn't have needed to bother with this murder investigation at all. That's why Max and I have been working so hard to figure out who killed Nathan O'Rourke, you know—Isabella gave me an ultimatum and told me if I didn't exonerate Christian before my wedding, then I would have to marry him and not Max."

Something about Lucy's posture altered

slightly, as if she thought she should try to back down but wasn't exactly sure how. "*That's* what's going on?"

"Yes," I said, knowing I needed to stop myself from telling her what a child she was being about all this. Doing so would definitely not earn me any points. "Christian seems like a very nice man, but Max is the only person I could ever possibly marry. And if I want to do that, then I need to make sure Christian is cleared of all charges."

"So if you've got any additional information you'd like to offer, now's the time," Max put in, clearly wanting to take advantage of Lucy's current indecision. "Believe me, Skye and I would like to get this whole mess cleared up sooner rather than later."

"I don't know anything," Lucy replied, her arms now crossed, an obviously self-defensive posture. "I mean, I heard about Christian punching that Nathan guy in the face, but that's about it. *I* definitely didn't have anything to do with it."

"Any idea why I might have seen your face in my dream, then?"

Something in Lucy's expression altered subtly, although, since I didn't know her at all well, I couldn't begin to decipher what the shadow that had crossed her features could possibly mean. "No," she said. "It sounds like your dream got its wires crossed. I know for a fact that I never met Nathan O'Rourke."

Even though I couldn't quite tell what had been going on with my half-sister a moment earlier, those last words of hers definitely had the ring of truth.

I glanced over at Max and noticed the way he was watching Lucy carefully, analyzing her every movement, every expression. Being an actor, he was probably used to studying people like that, trying to interpret their emotions and reactions so he could incorporate them in his own work as needed.

Maybe he'd gained some insights he could share later.

"I know," I said. "Alicia told me you weren't even in Las Vegas the night of the murder, which is why I guessed the dream had to be wrong. I just don't know what it was trying to tell me."

To my surprise, Lucy appeared almost sympathetic. "I wish I knew," she replied. "And it's awful what the great-aunts are trying to do to you. I think I'm going to try to talk to them, tell them this whole thing is silly and that they should just let me be with Christian the way I've always wanted."

"'Always'?" Max repeated, as though he wasn't quite sure he was willing to believe her on that point.

Once again, Lucy's dark eyes flashed fire, but she sounded civil enough as she said, "Okay, the last year or so. I mean, before that, I would have been too young, right?"

And Christian would have been too married, I thought, although I remained silent.

"Well, he seems like a nice guy," Max said. "I hope it works out for you two."

"Oh, it will," Lucy responded. "I'll make sure of it."

And without even a simple wave of her hand, she disappeared, leaving Max and me alone in the family room.

I couldn't help blinking. "So much for that," I remarked, then looked up at my fiancé. "Do you really think she'll be able to make the great-aunts see reason?"

The corners of his mouth quirked. "Normally, I'd say no, because they seem pretty set in their ways. But your little half-sister is kind of a force of nature, so who knows?"

I wished it could end that easily. If Lucy convinced the Petrucci elders to back down, then Max and I would have nothing to worry about. We could get married and go on with our lives.

No, scratch that. Not the getting married part, but I knew I wouldn't let this rest until Christian was a free man. After the tragedy he'd suffered in his life, it seemed like the least I could do. True, he'd have to deal with Lucy's unwanted attentions after that, but I figured that was a small price to pay for not spending the rest of his life behind bars.

"I guess we'll have to wait and see," I replied. "Even if Lucy somehow manages to prevail, I'm sure my great-aunts will derive some pleasure from torturing us by not letting us know until tomorrow morning."

That comment earned me an amused lift of Max's eyebrows. "You don't have a very high opinion of them, do you?"

"Why should I?" I retorted, and he let out a chuckle that was dangerously close to a snort.

"No reason," he said. "And I have to agree with you—they don't seem like a very reasonable bunch."

Since we were both on the same page when it came to the Petrucci elders, I figured it was time to move on to more important topics. "You were paying pretty close attention to Lucy just now. Did you pick up on anything weird?"

Max loosened his tie, then pulled it all the way off so he could set it on the coffee table. "I hate those things," he said to the room in general. "But Lucy? Yes, I felt like something was off for a minute there, but I couldn't begin to tell you why. Just instinct. I didn't get the feeling that she was lying, exactly, more...."

The words trailed off there, and his brows scrunched together as he apparently replayed the scene in his head, trying to figure out why my half-sister's comments hadn't felt quite right.

"More like she wasn't telling the whole truth," I supplied, and he nodded.

"That's it. Like she thought of something but didn't want to say anything to us, for whatever reason."

Which meant that, even if Lucy wasn't the murderer, she also wasn't someone we could trust. But I supposed that was the Petruccis for you...they seemed to be really good at keeping secrets.

Except Christian. Maybe my instincts were completely off-base on this—it wouldn't be the first time—and yet I couldn't help thinking he was someone who'd been in the wrong place at the wrong time and nothing more.

All the more reason why we needed to do our damnedest to make sure he was exonerated.

But dealing with Lucy's outburst on top of everything else that had gone on today reminded me of how tired I was. I supposed I might have a flash of inspiration if I forced myself to stay up until all hours, beating my head against all the facts we'd gathered in this murder case. More likely, though, I'd just end up exhausting myself, and for what?

Also, if by some miracle we were finally able to pierce through to the heart of the matter, I didn't want to have dark circles under my eyes in all my wedding photos.

That silly detail seemed to decide things. I put a hand on Max's knee and said, "I know we should probably keep working on this, but I feel like I'm about to fall over. Let's see if a good night's sleep will help us get some perspective on things."

"Good idea," he replied immediately. "I'm pretty beat, too. At least we have some more time."

Some time, yes.

But not enough.

To my infinite surprise, I actually slept well that night, as if my body had realized it needed to cut me some slack. No dreams, unfortunately, or at least, none that I could remember. In a way, though, that was a good thing. It seemed to reinforce my belief that the dream I'd had with Lucy in it had been true in some way, even if I hadn't yet been able to grasp exactly what it was trying to tell me. Otherwise, I would have had other dreams to follow it, dreams that would have muddied the waters.

Still, I knew I was tense as I sat down to breakfast that morning, although Lou had outdone himself with sourdough French toast and applewood-smoked bacon and a gorgeous fruit compote.

I knew I needed to eat because there would be precious little time for that sort of thing after I got to the hotel. True, I'd ordered a charcuterie board for Deanne and Darcy and me to nosh on while we were getting prepped, but I had a feeling it was going to be hard to pop pieces of cheese and meat in my mouth while I was getting worked on by a hairstylist and then a makeup artist.

I hadn't really wanted to go to those lengths to prepare for the wedding, but Deanne had insisted. "Do you want to look like some country bumpkin when your wedding photos are going to be published all over the world?" she'd asked, and I'd reluctantly agreed.

That meant Andie had stepped in with some recommendations for people she knew in Albuquerque and Santa Fe, and after that, I hired two hairdressers and two makeup artists to work on the three of us. I'd thought about getting more people, but Deanne had said that wasn't necessary, and that she and Darcy could make do with one stylist and one makeup artist for both of them.

At any rate, I had a feeling that once I got to the hotel, things were going to be chaotic at best. Normally, we wouldn't have been able to check in until after three, but the management had made an exception, considering the momentousness of the occasion, and we were now expected to show up at one.

I supposed that was handy...sort of. If I wasn't able to get Nathan's murder figured out by four o'clock, at least all I'd have to do was walk downstairs to the rooms where my great-aunts were staying and give them the news.

Because both Lou and Al wanted to be patrolling the perimeter of the property until Max and I were safely away, Lou set my breakfast plate in front of me, instructed me to eat up, and then headed outside. I'd been a little later coming into the kitchen than Max, so he had already eaten part of his French toast and one slice of bacon.

"You doing okay?" he asked as I reached for my cup of coffee.

"I think so," I replied. "I guess I'm just sort of... numb." I forced a lopsided smile, adding, "Probably not the best frame of mind to be in on my wedding day, but I suppose there are extenuating circumstances."

"There definitely are," he agreed. As he picked up a second piece of bacon, he asked, "Any dreams?"

"Nope," I said. "So I think that means the dream I had is the one I should be paying attention to. I just wish I knew what the hell it was supposed to mean."

Chewing thoughtfully, Max nodded. After he was done with his bite of bacon, he said, "In a way, that's a good thing. At least we're not dealing with even more clues we need to pick apart at the eleventh hour."

Maybe he was right, but still, I would have much preferred getting a healthy shot of inspiration. As it was, I felt as if I was blundering around in the fog more than ever.

However, I managed to eat a couple of bites of French toast and wash them down with some coffee, telling myself that Lou was right, that I needed to eat no matter how I was feeling, and maybe Max had the correct view of the situation as well, that it was good I didn't have to try deciphering a new dream just as the clock was ticking down.

Even though we didn't have anyone listening in to our conversation, we both seemed to understand we didn't have anything new to contribute to solving the mystery. That was why we talked about the reception, about the family we'd get to see, about our upcoming trip to Rome and Tuscany— about pretty much anything, in fact, other than Nathan O'Rourke and the person who had killed him.

I took a long, hot shower, and then got into a button-up shirt and my oldest, rattiest pair of jeans. It didn't matter what I looked like before I began my bridal transformation, and since Lita, the woman who was doing my hair, had informed me I needed to wear something I didn't have to pull over my head, I'd chosen an old chambray shirt with paint stains, figuring there wasn't anything we could do to it that hadn't been done already.

No makeup, either. What would be the point?

Because of that, I was ready way earlier than I needed to be. Max was on the phone with his publicist, going over a few details of the day. He sounded utterly calm, and not at all like someone whose wedding was about to go down the drain in a few short hours.

It's because he doesn't think that's really going to happen, I told myself. *Everything has always gone Max's way, and I don't think he can conceive of a situation where things don't work out okay in the end.*

Unfortunately, I knew happy endings weren't guaranteed. I wouldn't tell him that, though. Better to let him convince himself that we were going to pull this off at the last minute, like one of the action heroes he always played, defusing a bomb just as it counted down to its last second.

He drove me over to the hotel and dropped me off; the groomsmen also had a changing room of their own at the Plaza, but because it wasn't going to take them nearly as long to get ready, they didn't plan to meet up until closer to three.

"Call me if you think of anything," he told me as the Bronco rolled to a stop at the curb. "I'll also be racking my brains. But I'll be back around a quarter to three. After that...well, after that, we'll do what we have to."

I nodded. My throat was so tight right then, I didn't know what I would've sounded like if I'd tried to speak. As it was, I reached over and squeezed his hand, then got out of the SUV and hurried up the steps into the hotel. Several celebrity photographers were lurking, but since Max had put Gordon on guard duty in front of the Plaza against this very eventuality, I managed to get inside without too much trouble.

Deanne had already texted me to let me know she and Darcy were in Room 314, so I climbed the steps to the third floor. Although the hotel's elevator had generally behaved itself since its hiccups when it had dropped several floors almost a year ago, I still preferred to take the stairs, just to be safe.

I also spared a glance for Room 310 as I passed, smiling a little despite myself. That room had once been the office of Byron T. Wells, one of the early owners of the hotel. The room was widely known to be haunted, and although I'd never seen the ghost, I thought I'd sensed his presence up here on the Plaza's third floor when I was trying to figure out why the spectral activity in the Plaza had ramped up as the hundredth anniversary of the basement boiler explosion approached.

No sign of him today, though...not that I'd

expected there to be. Instead, everything seemed quiet enough.

Well, except for the sound of Deanne and Darcy's laughter coming from underneath the door to Room 314, along with a faint drift of Taylor Swift's "Shake It Off." I knocked, and Deanne opened the door a minute later, still looking cheerful.

"Bride's here!" she announced as she let me in.

At once, Lita, the hairstylist who would be working on me, hurried over. "We need to get started right away," she said, eyeing me critically. "You have a lot of hair."

Well, I supposed I did. And if I'd been thinking about anything else except my dilemma with the Petrucci witches, I might have tried to get here a little earlier, just so Lita would have more time to work on me.

I made a neutral sound and let her guide me to the station she'd set up, with a makeup mirror and swivel chair and lots of styling tools and power strips. In fact, there were so many curling irons held in their little swirled metal "holsters" that I barely avoided tripping over the cords.

However, I managed to land in the styling chair without causing too much mayhem, and Lita got to work at once. Darcy had called out a hello from where she was sitting, but because she already had a chunk of hair wrapped around a big-barrel curling iron as Rachel, the other stylist, worked on her, she couldn't do much more than that.

Finished with her own doorman duties, Deanne went over to the third chair and sat down so Ginny, the makeup artist, could go back to work on her. Because those two seats were placed closer together, she and Darcy had more opportunity for conversation, while I, isolated on the other side of the room, mostly had to sit there with my growing anxiety, shoulders in knots and stomach churning, as the minutes ticked past. True, when my two bridesmaids got a chance to switch places, Deanne came over and handed me a glass of champagne, along with a few bites from the charcuterie board that had been set up on top of the dresser.

"Here's to a fabulous day!" she exclaimed, and clinked her champagne flute against mine. Judging by the way her smile was just a little sloppy, I had a feeling she was already working on her second glass.

Which was fine. She still looked mostly in control of herself, and perfectly able to walk down an aisle. Actually, it was probably a good thing that Deanne was a little tipsy...it might soften the blow when Max and I had to call the whole thing off and submit to the Petrucci elders' wishes.

Somehow, I managed to smile back at my best friend and not be too obvious about the way my gaze slid toward the clock radio on the hotel room's nightstand.

Three fifteen, and I still had no idea who had murdered Nathan O'Rourke...and I kind of doubted that Max, who should be arriving soon so he could get changed into his wedding suit, had been struck by any bolts of inspiration in my absence.

I vaguely realized that Lita had switched places with Ginny, who was now dabbing on foundation and powder and doing complicated things with a contour palette. As I sat there, an overwhelming sense of futility came over me.

Well, at least I'd be looking my best when my doom fell...kind of like those French aristocrats wearing their silk finery as they were carted off to the guillotine.

A few minutes before four, Ginny stepped away, looking pleased with herself. She was about ten years older than I was, with bleached hair she wore in a pixie cut and dramatic dark brows. "You look amazing," she said. "Perfect for the cover of a magazine."

I didn't want to look good for a magazine. I wanted to look good for Max.

A little trepidatious, I peered into the mirror. At first, I barely recognized the glossy-looking woman with the huge dark eyes and perfectly sculpted cheekbones, then realized that truly was me. Or at least, the "me" that Rachel had turned me into.

"It looks great," I said, even as I thought that all her effort would soon be for nothing. "And my hair, too, Lita."

She nodded, also looking pleased. "You have gorgeous hair," she replied. "It was fun to work with."

I really didn't know whether I could call my hair "gorgeous," since it mostly did whatever it wanted despite my best efforts. However, it was thick and wavy and fell midway down my back, and looked pretty spectacular pulled up into an artfully messy bun with a couple of strategic strands falling around my face.

Deanne and Darcy came close, and oohed and aahed and told me Max was the luckiest guy in the world. I somehow managed to summon a smile from somewhere, even as my heart sank to roughly around my feet.

Caught up in the moment, they didn't seem to notice anything off, but helped me climb out of my sloppy outfit and into the gown I'd chosen, which was a dead-simple strapless dress made of ivory silk shantung. It clung to my body but wasn't too tight, and had a very modest train, something I could loop up at the reception to keep it out of the way while I was dancing.

Not that there was going to be a reception...or a wedding to precede it.

Swallowing past the lump in my throat, I said,

"Do you two mind heading downstairs while I hang here for a minute? I just kind of want to get myself centered."

Neither Darcy nor Deanne seemed to see anything odd about this request, because they only nodded and said I could meet them down in the lobby. The photographer had wanted to take pictures of the entire wedding party before the ceremony, but I'd declined, saying I didn't want Max to see me until I was walking down the aisle. We'd compromised on having some photos of me and my two attendants taken a little after four, which was why we were all supposed to congregate downstairs.

"Sure," Deanne said, while our hairstylists and makeup artists hurried out. They'd need to come back for their things after we were all out of here, but they'd obviously guessed I needed some alone time. "Just don't take too long."

"Five minutes," I promised, which was a flat-out lie. I wouldn't be going to the lobby at all.

No, once my two bridesmaids were safely out of the way, I'd need to head down one floor to meet the Petrucci elders.

Darcy and Deanne went out, leaving me alone in the room. It was utter chaos in there, what with our discarded street clothes still lying on the bed and all the makeup cases and styling tools scattered on the various tables, but it was the best I had right then.

You can do this, I told myself, and pulled in a deep breath. Unfortunately, it didn't seem to do much except make me feel a little dizzy, although that could have had something to do with the half glass of champagne I'd just drunk.

Problem was, I really didn't think I *could* do this. There had been people all throughout history who'd walked calmly to meet their fates, but I didn't appear to be one of them.

Someone knocked at the door, and I frowned. True, it was only a couple of minutes until four, but really, my great-aunts were being so hasty that they'd decided to jump the gun?

Frowning, I went over to the door and opened it...only to be confronted by a man I'd never seen before, tall and with dark hair and eyes, and features that looked oddly familiar.

However, I didn't get any more chance than that to analyze his face, because he lunged for me even as he slammed the door behind him.

"Interfering bitch!" he growled, hands outstretched...hands that looked as though they were ready to wrap around my throat.

I leaped backward—that is, I tried to dodge out of the way, tripped over my train, and barely managed to avoid careening into one of the little tray tables Lita had left behind. "Get away from me!" I screeched, stumbling like a drunk around the foot of the bed. "Who the hell do you think you are?"

"The man who's making sure his sister gets what she wants," he said, taking a menacing step toward me.

His *sister?* Who the hell was his sister?

And then it hit me like the proverbial bolt out of the blue.

Lucy Petrucci. The woman who wanted Christian...the man the elders were about to force me to marry.

And that meant my assailant had to be Luke, the half-brother I'd never met.

"I don't *want* to marry Christian!" I shot back. "If there's anyone you should be trying to throttle, it's your interfering great-aunts!"

He came closer, now looking almost smug, as if he knew he had me cornered and so could take his time. "But they're not the ones who are going to be Christian's wife," Luke countered. "With you out of the way, Lucy will be able to persuade them to let her marry Christian instead."

I severely doubted they would cave so easily, but the glitter in Luke's dark eyes—eyes that were way too similar to mine—told me he wasn't about to back down. Those black depths held the promise of all kinds of mayhem...and were probably the last thing Nathan O'Rourke had seen before he died.

The truth had finally caught up with me. Too bad I didn't know what the hell I was going to do with it.

Before I could respond, Luke had lunged forward again, this time catching me by the arm and pulling me toward him. I didn't even stop to think, but reached out for the nearest weapon that came to hand—in this case, one of the curling irons Lita had left in its little metal holster.

Swinging it by its cord, I smashed it into the side of Luke's face. He yelped, the red mark the whirling curling iron had left behind telling me the thing had still been hot enough to hurt quite a bit. In all the chaos, Lita must have forgotten to turn it off.

Unfortunately, the blow didn't stop Luke, but only appeared to enrage him that much further. His other hand reached up to grab my neck, fingers tightening.

I gasped for air and couldn't seem to gulp any down. Luke was tall and slender, and didn't look like someone who could possibly be this strong. The red spots dancing in front of my eyes seemed to tell me he was plenty strong enough to choke the life out of me right here and now if I didn't do something fast.

Now I needed to knock him out...just like he

himself had bludgeoned Nathan O'Rourke to death a week ago.

The mirror with all its vanity lights that Lita had brought with the rest of her gear flew up from where it sat on a table and rocketed across the room, smacking into Luke's head with a tremendous *cr-ack!* and sending bits of flying glass and light bulbs everywhere. At once, he slumped to the floor...

...and grabbed my ankle, pulling me down as well. By some miracle, my silk gown didn't split, although my hair escaped from the bun Lita had spent so much time constructing and went flying into my eyes, halfway blinding me.

What was up with this guy? Was there some kind of Michael Myers murdering gene in my family that I didn't know about?

I kicked out, catching him in the throat with one of my satin kitten-heel pumps. He gasped, one hand going up to cover the wound, which was already starting to pump out blood.

And then the door to the hotel room was flung open, and I saw Max reach down and grab Luke Petrucci by the collar before tossing him against the wall like a rag doll. This time, my evil half-brother hit the floor and stayed there, even as Max hurried over to me and raised me to my feet.

"Are you okay, Skye? What happened?"

"I'm all right," I said, and nodded toward the

prone form of my assailant, who definitely looked as though he was down for the count. "That's Luke, Lucy's brother. He's the one who murdered Nathan...and who almost just murdered me."

Max's eyes widened, but at least he had enough presence of mind to pull his phone out of his jacket pocket and hit the 9-1-1 button. He said, "There's a suspected murderer in Room 314 at the Plaza Hotel," then returned the phone to his pocket before the person on the other end of the line could respond. "Well," he said, "it looks like we're going to have a wedding after all."

Despite the crazy Petruccis.

I reached out to take his hand, to feel how real and strong and *there* his fingers were. At the same time, I couldn't avoid catching a glimpse of my reflection in one of the mirrors that remained. My hair was falling down all over the place, and one of my false eyelashes had been knocked askew.

"We are," I said with a grin. "But first, I think we need a little cleanup on Aisle Five."

CHAPTER 17

All's Well

A ll things considered, I thought it was a pretty good reflection of Max's and my resiliency that the wedding was only postponed by about forty-five minutes. The police came and hauled Luke away, and although Marie DeVargas was full of questions, she made sure that taking our statement didn't use up more than ten minutes of our precious time. Repairing the damage my half-brother had done to my hair and makeup took a bit longer, but still, at a little before six o'clock, Max and I were finally able to exchange our vows.

Without my mother or my half-sister or any of the Petrucci aunts in attendance, which was fine by me. They'd all gone to the police station to see about bailing out Luke, telling me everything I needed to know about where their allegiances lay.

Not that I cared. I'd never asked for them to be

in my life, and I was all too happy to think this latest incident would make sure they'd stay well out of it from now on.

Well, except for the part where I'd have to testify against Luke in court, whenever that happened.

For now, though, I was just happy to have Max standing there and gazing down at me with all the love in the world in his eyes, and to know he'd always be there for me...yes, up to and including saving my life.

The story got around, of course, and I had to spend a good chunk of the reception telling everyone that yes, I was fine, and wild horses—or sociopathic relatives—weren't enough to keep me from marrying Max Sullivan.

"You really are my knight in shining armor," I told him as we danced our first dance to the sultry sounds of Etta James crooning "At Last," his arms sure and strong around me, his mere presence letting me know that finally, against all odds, my dreams had actually come true.

He bent and laid a soft kiss on the top of my head. "I don't know—it looked like you were doing a pretty good job of defending yourself. How'd you manage to throw that mirror at Luke's head?"

A very good question. Since I didn't know exactly what had happened, I really couldn't say. "I don't know," I responded. "It just flew through the air and smacked into him."

"Your magic at work?" Max asked, and I gave a little shrug.

"Maybe," I said. "But it wasn't anything I did consciously. It just sort of...happened."

"It makes sense. Your magic knew you were in danger, so it acted out to protect you."

That was as good a theory as any, I supposed. Since I didn't have a conscious recollection of doing so, I decided to roll with it now in the absence of any other theories.

It was still strange, though. My magic had never done anything like that before, so I didn't quite know what to believe...and I honestly didn't like the idea that it might decide on its own when I needed protecting.

But that niggling doubt was easy enough to push aside when I was having such a good time, especially when I reminded myself that even I didn't have the opportunity to be attacked by murderous half-brothers very often. Everyone at the reception seemed to be sharing in the happy vibes, including Kyle and Andie, who danced three dances in a row together and ended up sitting in a corner, talking, for most of the night.

Well, maybe I'd have a career ahead of me as a matchmaker rather than baking muffins.

The evening started to wind down around

eleven, and I noticed how Andie and Kyle left hand in hand, still chatting and smiling. Everyone hugged me and Max and congratulated us, although Deanne had that look in her eyes that told me she wanted explanations, and soon. She hadn't pressed me too much at the reception because there were so many other people claiming my attention, but I knew sooner or later, I'd need to spill the whole story to her.

Exactly when that was supposed to happen, I didn't know for sure, because we planned to leave in the morning to catch the flight that would be the first leg of our journey to Rome.

As Lou was driving us back to the ranch—Max and I had both decided it was silly to hire a limo, although my Texas cousins had orchestrated a nice collection of tin cans and old shoes to be tied to the Bronco's rear bumper—Max leaned over and said, "We don't have to leave right away, you know."

I blinked at him, startled. "What...no honeymoon?"

"That's not what I meant." He'd already been holding my hand, but he gave it a little squeeze now, the diamonds in the second band he'd slipped on my finger earlier glittering even in the low light inside the SUV's back seat. "Just...delay things a little. Can you honestly say you want to fly out of here tomorrow and not find out what's going on with Luke and the rest of your family?"

No, I really couldn't, because the same thought had been dancing around in the back of my mind during most of the reception, like an annoying fly that wouldn't stop hovering over an especially luscious picnic basket. "Well...." I said, then chuckled. "Okay, you got me on that one. It'll feel like we didn't get closure if we leave tomorrow. But what about all our travel plans?"

"I'll text Courtney when we get home and let her know what we want to do. Maybe bump everything back two weeks? We'd be going to Rome in the middle of May instead, which should be gorgeous. And I don't have to start my next shoot until the end of June, so we'll still have plenty of time to come back home and relax afterward."

He really had been thinking about it. Courtney had come to Las Vegas for the wedding, so she was back at the hotel. Even though it was getting late, I doubted she'd gone to bed yet.

And even if she was, well, I doubted this would be the first time she'd gotten a late-night text from her boss. Max definitely didn't abuse his assistant like some Hollywood stars did, but he was also used to getting things handled when he needed them handled.

That was why she responded with an immediate, *On it,* when he messaged her after we got home, and why I knew we wouldn't have any need of the luggage that was waiting for us in the master suite.

Well, not any time during the next two weeks, that is.

WHEN IT GOT TO BE A DECENT HOUR THE next morning, I called Deanne and told her Max and I were staying put in Las Vegas until the dust settled from Luke's arrest. She was full of questions, as I'd expected, but I didn't have a lot of answers.

With any luck, that was something that would be rectified in the very near future.

Before I could decide whether to call Kyle to get the skinny on Luke Petrucci's current legal status or whether I should wait a while in case he was spending the morning with Andie, my phone rang. At that point, Max and I were sitting out on the patio, drinking iced tea and discussing whether we should go horseback riding or possibly run up to Taos for the day, since the weather was so nice.

But the number on the display was Alicia's, and I knew I needed to answer.

"It's Alicia," I told Max, and he nodded at once.

"Then I'll let you take it," he said, and got up

from his chair. "Just come get me when you're done."

He bent and kissed me, not a lingering kiss, but still passionate enough to evoke all the wonderful things we'd done the evening before to celebrate our first night together as husband and wife. I did my best to suppress the flare of heat that went through my body, since that wasn't the kind of state I wanted to be in while having this conversation with my mother.

"Hi, Alicia," I said, praying I sounded normal and not as though I'd wanted to put down my phone and tear off my husband's clothes just a moment earlier. "How are you holding up?"

"As well as can be expected," she replied. Her voice sounded both tight and flat, and not at all like herself. "Luke is in jail until Monday, when a judge will decide on his bail. Our attorney says it isn't looking very good, though, not with him being accused of both murder and attempted murder."

"They found evidence linking him to Nathan O'Rourke's murder?" I asked, startled. After all, I'd known without a shadow of a doubt that Luke was the killer, but it wasn't as though I had any concrete proof.

A small silence. Then, "It sounds that way. They searched his room at the Castañeda and found a baseball bat with Mr. O'Rourke's DNA on it."

Her voice caught then, and, despite everything Alicia had put me through, I couldn't hold back the wave of pity I felt for her. She'd made a lot of mistakes in her life, but that didn't mean she deserved to deal with the trauma of a son who'd turned out to be a stone-cold killer.

As to why Luke had held onto the bat rather than flinging it out into the wilderness somewhere, I couldn't say. Maybe he'd thought no one would ever trace the murder to him, and it seemed safer to keep the bat in his possession rather than leave its discovery up to fate. Maybe he'd been so arrogant that he'd believed the long arm of the law would never reach his way.

"I'm sorry," I said, and meant it. Not for Luke, but for the wake of destruction he'd left behind him.

She didn't reply immediately, although I thought I heard her breath catch, and guessed she was probably doing her best to hold back tears. "Lucy's been crying all night," Alicia said after a pause. "We all kept telling her this wasn't her fault, but she seems to think Luke would never have acted out if he hadn't been trying to protect her, to protect the family. He's not talking to the police, and he hasn't said much to us, only that he was trying to make Lucy happy. They were always very close, you know."

I didn't know, since I'd only just met them. But

I remembered how Alicia had said much the same thing a few days earlier, how she'd referred to them as her "Irish twins" because they'd been born less than a year apart.

Twins....

Of course. That was what the tea leaves had been trying to tell me. No, Luke and Lucy weren't actual twins, but they might as well have been. The tea leaves had shown me that image twice because they wanted me to know the killer was connected to someone who thought of his sister as a twin.

"I can understand why he'd come after me," I said slowly. "But I still don't understand why Luke thought he needed to kill Nathan O'Rourke."

"Because Mr. O'Rourke was going to sue Christian," Alicia replied. "Doing so would have made Lucy unhappy—not to mention bringing scrutiny upon the family that we really couldn't afford—so Luke decided to take matters into his own hands." Another of those tense little pauses, and she added, "And I'm afraid I helped him."

"You?" I said, astonished. For all of Alicia's character flaws, I still couldn't exactly see her as an accessory to murder.

"Not directly," she said. "But I realized he must have used my car when he killed Mr. O'Rourke. I could tell someone had driven it, even though I had no idea how or why. That must have been how he moved the body from...well, from wherever it happened...to Mr. O'Rourke's car in that parking lot."

So, Luke had skills in stealing cars in addition to committing bodily mayhem?

The truth, however, was much simpler.

"He and Lucy both have key fobs for the BMW," Alicia explained. "They rarely used them, although Luke drove the car for a few days last summer while his was in the shop for a factory recall. Anyway, Lucy confessed that she brought Luke here to Las Vegas last week when I thought he was still in New York. He must have taken the car while I was asleep that night. The only reason I noticed anything was because he forgot to readjust the driver's seat after he was done."

I guessed that Alicia's fancy BMW had programmed settings for each of the people who drove it regularly, which meant Luke must have been in a hell of a hurry when he dropped it off last Friday night. Not too surprising, I supposed; committing murder had to be nerve-shattering even for someone whose moral code didn't have a problem with mayhem if it meant saving the family name.

"And the great-aunts?"

Now the sigh that came through the phone's speaker was clearly audible. "Oh, they've already gone back to New York. They've done their work, so they don't feel as if there's any point in staying here."

"'Done their work'?" I repeated, thinking that phrase sounded awfully ominous. "What does that mean?"

"It means the three of them wove a spell that drove any memory of the Petruccis as a witch family out of Luke's mind," Alicia said. "Luke doesn't have any powers of his own, obviously, but there was always the chance he might let something slip. The elders couldn't allow that, so they simply got rid of those memories."

I doubted there was anything "simple" about it. Despite the warm sun shining down on me, a shiver wriggled its way along my spine.

Obviously, my great-aunts didn't scruple at much if it meant keeping the Petrucci secrets safe... and they had the powers to make it happen.

"And Christian?" I asked. Maybe I should have left it alone, but it sure seemed to me like he was the innocent bystander in all this.

"Oh, he left with the elders after the charges against him were dropped. I suppose my aunts decided they owed him a fast trip back to New York after everything he'd gone through."

It was on the tip of my tongue to ask whether Alicia thought Christian would ever forgive Lucy for the damage her infatuation had caused, then decided it was better to let it go. He was probably processing a lot, and not really in a position right now to make decisions about his future.

"I'm surprised the elders didn't spirit Luke away, too," I remarked, and Alicia actually chuckled. Or at least, the sound she made in response to my comment sounded partly amused.

"No, that would have raised far too many questions. Better to let Luke meet his fate now that there's no chance of him betraying the family."

"What about you?" I asked. "Are you going to stay here in case he posts bail?"

Her answer was immediate, firm. "He won't post bail. And I won't be staying. No, Lucy and I are going home so we can pick up the pieces and see our way forward from here." She broke off then, waited a second or two, and went on. "As I know you will, too. I hope you and Max have a very happy life together."

The call ended abruptly there, and I put the phone down.

I had a feeling I wouldn't hear from her again.

———

THE NEWS GOT AROUND SWIFTLY ENOUGH that Max and I had postponed our honeymoon, but people seemed to understand why we'd wanted to stick around a while longer. I told Deanne the entire bonkers story, and she just shook her head.

"Luke must really be crazy," she said, and about all I could do was shrug.

I didn't know for sure that he was crazy, at least not in any way that could be confirmed by a psychiatrist. Clearly, though, his loyalty to his sister had superseded any other claims on his emotions... which was probably part of the reason why he'd been having trouble with his wife.

Alicia's suspicions were confirmed when Luke was denied bail. It seemed the Petruccis were providing him enough support that he wouldn't have to rely on a public defender, but it didn't sound as though any of them planned to return for his trial, which had been set for the end of June. I wished he could have gone to court, been sentenced, and shipped off to a maximum-security prison before then, although Kyle assured me he wasn't getting out.

"We have someone watching him twenty-four seven," he informed me when he came into the coffee shop the Thursday after the wedding. I'd thought about keeping Levitation Latte closed the whole time but eventually decided that wouldn't be fair to the people who were already feeling deprived of their caffeine fix. That was why I'd decided to reopen with limited hours, operating from nine in the morning to three in the afternoon. True, the people who relied on getting my coffee on the way to work were out of luck, but I could still help anyone who came in during their morning break, or who wanted a pick-me-up at lunch.

The news from Kyle reassured me a bit. Not all the way, but enough that I hoped Luke wouldn't be a continuing problem. I probably would have been a lot more worried if it weren't painfully obvious that the Petruccis had jettisoned him in an effort to keep their secrets safe. If I'd been at all close to my mother, I might have tried to find out how she felt about the way the family had written off her son, but as it was, I could only hope they'd continue to stay far, far out of my life...and away from Las Vegas.

It was on the tip of my tongue to ask Kyle how things were going with Andie, although I decided to hold my tongue for now. They'd seemed very chummy the night of the reception and I hoped they were continuing to see each other, and yet it really didn't feel like my place to ask.

He thanked me for the coffee and muffin and headed out, and there went that opportunity.

However, I was startled the next day to see Andie come in late in the afternoon, right before closing. She was wearing jeans and a pretty top and flats, making me think she probably wasn't here on official business...not that there was much in the way of that kind of business for her in Las Vegas. People had been effusive about the food and the wedding cake, but the sad truth was that not many residents of my hometown could really afford to hire her to cater their special events.

"Hey, there," I said as Andie came up to the counter. Deanne had already left, since she'd scheduled a doctor's appointment for that afternoon, thinking she wouldn't be working at all this week. "I wasn't expecting to see you in Las Vegas again so soon."

A bit of pink dusted Andie's cheeks. "Well... Kyle and I have a date," she said. "He's off at five today, and he doesn't have to work again until Monday. For once, I have a weekend free, so I thought this was the perfect time for some rest and relaxation."

She'd said "date" and hadn't mentioned anything about staying with Kyle, but I could read between the lines. It sure looked as though matters between them were progressing a lot faster than I'd expected.

"That sounds like fun," I replied. "I'm glad you could get away. The weather's perfect for hiking and roaming around."

"We're planning on doing that...and spending some time tomorrow at the hot springs," she said. "It'll be fun to get to know Las Vegas a little more. I really like this town."

Something she'd already told me, but it seemed

she was appreciating our little piece of perfection a bit more every time she visited.

"Have you ever thought about moving here?" I blurted out.

Rather than give me a glance that told me I was way out of line, she nodded. "Crazy, right? I was even looking on Zillow for rentals this past week. But there just isn't much available right now, especially with the kind of kitchen I need."

Sometimes, the universe made sure everyone was in the right place at the right time...and I guessed this was one of those times.

"You could rent my house," I said, and Andie blinked, obviously startled. Before she could say anything, though, I went on, "It's been sitting there empty ever since I moved in with Max, but I couldn't quite bring myself to put it on the market. But I'd love to rent it to you—I updated the place a few years ago, and the kitchen's set up for cooking and baking. It's four bedrooms and two baths, and just a squidge under 2,400 square feet."

"Sounds perfect," Andie replied, hope and doubt warring in her expression. I couldn't blame her...it truly did sound too good to be true. "And you'd really be okay with renting it to me?"

"I can't think of anyone better," I told her. "It's yours, if you want it."

She was silent for a moment, during which I had a feeling her practical side was battling with instincts that told her to just go for it. "I do," she said firmly. "It somehow feels right, you know?"

"I do," I said. "It's furnished, but I can have everything moved to storage if you've got your own stuff."

Now her hazel eyes danced with amusement. "My 'stuff' consists of a few pieces I ordered online because I didn't want to sit on the floor, but it's nothing I can't sell before I move. I'd love a furnished house."

Because I'd worked with her, I knew how meticulous she was about everything, how careful and attentive to details. She would take good care of the place...and I had a feeling my grandmother would approve of my solution for what to do with the property.

"Then it's a done deal," I said. "I'll put together a lease—just let me know when you can move in."

"Middle of next week?" she responded, now looking a little dazed. "I've got an event on Saturday, so I'd like to get it handled before then."

"Perfect. Max and I are flying out the following Monday, so we'll be here to help you get settled and sort out anything that needs to be fixed before we leave."

Face glowing, Andie thanked me and said she was looking forward to getting the lease signed. "Kyle's going to be surprised," she remarked.

That was for sure. However, I had a sneaking suspicion he would be just fine with the situation.

But there was someone else I needed to check in with first.

Tilly was lapping water in the back room when I stuck my head in, her ears laid back, telling me she'd probably overheard my entire conversation with Andie and wasn't too thrilled about it.

"You're giving that woman your house?" the cat demanded.

"I'm not 'giving' it to her," I said. "I'm renting it. Besides, what do you care? You haven't been there in ages."

"No," Tilly said slowly, "but I sort of liked knowing it was there, just in case."

"Well, you can always come live with Max and me at the ranch," I offered. "It's kind of silly that you haven't."

The cat's green eyes narrowed. "There are coyotes out there."

Something I couldn't really dispute, because I'd heard them crying to the moon on more than one occasion. "True," I said. "But it's not like they come in the house."

Something close to horror registered on Tilly's feline features. "You want me to be a house cat? No way."

About what I'd thought she'd say, since she'd steadfastly refused to go to the ranch all these months. "Well, then, you can stay here. Deanne will come in to take care of you while Max and I are out of town, so nothing is really going to change that much. But my offer to come to the ranch is always open to you."

A brief silence while Tilly appeared to consider my words. "Okay," she said grudgingly. "I don't really like you giving your house away, but as long as I can be here at the shop, I suppose it's all right."

"Then that's settled," I said, and Tilly gave the cat equivalent of a shrug.

"Guess so."

After that, she disappeared out the cat door, putting an end to the conversation. She always had come and gone as she pleased, and I knew she'd never give up her ability to roam Las Vegas's downtown, the only life she'd ever known.

When I got home, Max was equally startled by the news I had to share, but then he gave me an approving hug and kiss. "I'm so glad you got the house figured out," he told me. "I know you were still worried about what you should do with it."

"I honestly can't think of anyone else I'd want living there," I replied. "Andie's going to cook and bake and stay true to the spirit of the house. So, that's taken care of."

Max reached over and took my hand. "And maybe...maybe after she's been here in Las Vegas for a while, you might want to see if she's interested in the coffee shop."

"'The coffee shop'?" I repeated.

Of course. We hadn't made a decision yet about whether I should keep running the business or whether I should give it up so I'd have more freedom to travel with Max. Since things had been so crazy lately, thanks to the mess with the Petruccis and the wedding planning, I really hadn't had enough time to sit down and think about what I wanted to do, but I could see where my husband was going with this.

Who better than a master cook and baker to take over the business? She could even turn it into a real restaurant if she wanted, instead of having to be up at the crack of dawn to bake muffins and pastries. Some people might not be completely happy with the change, but really, there were more coffee shops in Las Vegas than decent restaurants. It might be nice for us to have a real fine dining option.

Of course, I'd also have to let her know that the business included its own talking cat, but that could wait until we got things well and truly settled.

"I'll mention it to Andie after she moves in," I said, once I'd mulled over Max's suggestion for a few moments. "I don't want to hit her with everything at once."

"That sounds like a plan," he replied, then pulled me closer to him so he could give me another kiss, this one warm and lingering, telling me he'd thought of several ways we could amuse ourselves before it was time to get dinner together. He paused there, however, scanning my face, as though to reassure himself I really was on board with the idea. "And you don't mind giving up Levitation Latte? I definitely don't want to force you into something you don't want to do."

I didn't reply at first, since I wanted to give myself the time to really think about what all this meant. For so many years, the coffee shop had been my identity, the thing that had given my life shape and meaning. The situation had changed now, and I wanted the freedom to explore a new life with Max, to be able to do all the things I never could before.

My fingers crept into his, and I squeezed them gently. "This feels right," I said. "I want to go with you to Rome next week, and to your shoot in Ireland in June. I want to be able to travel and see all the things I haven't gotten to see before now." I went on my toes and pressed a kiss against his cheek, hoping he could feel in the soft brush of skin against skin how much I wanted all of this... wanted him. "I want to have adventures with you, Max."

He bent and kissed me again, and another thrill

went through my body. "I think we've had plenty of adventures already," he said, the corners of his luscious mouth quirking a bit. "I understand, though. Let's have the right kind of adventures together."

"And no more murders," I said firmly, and he laughed.

"No, my love," he said, "no more murders."

The End

This marks the end of the Levitation and Lattes series. For more cozy mysteries from Christine Pope, check out her Hedgewitch for Hire and Familiar Spirits series, or turn the page to see all her books!

Also by Christine Pope

THE DJINN WARS

(Paranormal Romance)

Chosen

Taken

Fallen

Broken

Forsaken

Forbidden

Awoken

Illuminated

Stolen

Forgotten

Driven

Unspoken

Hidden

Written (May 2024)

Given (August 2024)

FAMILIAR SPIRITS

(Cozy Mystery/Paranormal Romance)

Spells and Spaniels

Cauldrons and Cats

Hexes and Hedgehogs

Charms and Chihuahuas (April 2024)

LATTES AND LEVITATION

(Cozy Mystery/Paranormal Romance)

Caffeine Before Curses

Muffins After Magic

Pastries and Prophecies

Eclairs and Ectoplasm

Sugar Skulls and Specters

Wedding Cakes and Wishes

HEDGEWITCH FOR HIRE

(Cozy Mystery/Paranormal Romance)

Grave Mistake

Social Medium

Household Demons

Perpetual Potion

Jingle Spells

Wandering Monsters

Uninvited Ghosts

Prophet Motive

Ballroom Bits

Spell Check

Brew Confessions (February 2024)

UNEXPECTED MAGIC*

(Urban Fantasy/Paranormal Romance)

Found Objects

Finders, Keepers

Lost and Found

Finding Destiny

THE WITCHES OF WHEELER PARK*

(Paranormal Romance)

Storm Born

Thunder Road

Winds of Change

Mind Games

A Wheeler Park Christmas

Blood Ties

Healing Hands

Wishful Thinking

Smoke and Mirrors

MISS PRIMM'S ACADEMY FOR WAYWARD
WITCHES*

(Fantasy/Academy Romance)

Misspelled

Dispelled

Expelled

PROJECT DEMON HUNTERS*

(Paranormal Romance)

Unquiet Souls

Unbound Spirits

Unholy Ground

Unseen Voices

Unmarked Graves

Unbroken Vows

THE DEVIL YOU KNOW*

(Paranormal Romance)

Sympathy for the Devil

Charmed, I'm Sure

A Wing and a Prayer

Wish Upon a Star

THE WITCHES OF CANYON ROAD*

(Paranormal Romance)

Hidden Gifts

Darker Paths

Mysterious Ways

A Canyon Road Christmas

Demon Born

An Ill Wind

Higher Ground

Haunted Hearts

THE WITCHES OF CLEOPATRA HILL*

(Paranormal Romance)

Darkangel

Darknight

Darkmoon

Sympathetic Magic

Protector

Spellbound

A Cleopatra Hill Christmas

Impractical Magic

Strange Magic

The Arrangement

Defender

Bad Blood

Deep Magic

Darktide

THE WATCHERS TRILOGY*

(Paranormal Romance)

Falling Dark

Dead of Night

Rising Dawn

THE SEDONA FILES*

(Paranormal/Science Fiction Romance)

Bad Vibrations

Desert Hearts

Angel Fire

Star Crossed

Falling Angels

Enemy Mine

TALES OF THE LATTER KINGDOMS*

(Fantasy Romance)

All Fall Down

Dragon Rose

Binding Spell

Ashes of Roses

One Thousand Nights

Threads of Gold

The Wolf of Harrow Hall

Moon Dance

The Song of the Thrush

THE GAIAN CONSORTIUM SERIES*

(Science Fiction Romance)

Beast (free prequel novella)

Blood Will Tell

Breath of Life

The Gaia Gambit

The Mandala Maneuver

The Titan Trap

The Zhore Deception

The Refugee Ruse

STANDALONE TITLES

Hearts on Fire (Paranormal Romance)

Taking Dictation (Contemporary Romance)

Golden Heart (Gaslight Fantasy Romance)

Night Music: A Modern Reimagining of The Phantom
of the Opera (Contemporary Romance)

Ghost Dance: A Sequel to Gaston Leroux's The
Phantom of the Opera (Historical Mystery/Romance)

Flight Before Christmas (Fantasy Romance)

* Indicates a completed series

About the Author

USA Today bestselling author Christine Pope has been writing stories ever since she commandeered her family's Smith-Corona typewriter back in grade school. Her work includes paranormal romance, cozy paranormal mystery, and urban fantasy, among others. She makes her home in New Mexico.

Christine Pope on the Web:
www.christinepope.com

facebook.com/ChristinePopeAuthor
pinterest.com/ChristineJPope
bookbub.com/authors/christine-pope

www.ingramcontent.com/pod-product-compliance
Lightning Source LLC
Chambersburg PA
CBHW020406260626
47156CB00007B/2252